COMMITTAL

a novel

IRENE COOPER

A woman in the shape of a monster
a monster in the shape of a woman
the skies are full of them

~Adrienne Rich, "Planetarium"

WESTHAVEN

The child lay on a white sheet on the table.

The doctor gripped the blond beechwood handle, stained tawny with age and perspiration, and swirled the instrument in a final revolution before removing its eight-centimeter steel spike from the girl's prefrontal cortex, soft as butter, and out her eye socket. He lay it beside its viscous twin on a cream lace cloth covering a mahogany sideboard, next to a small electric console from which two wires emerged, ending in the pair of round discs that echoed the half dollar bruises on the girl's pale temples.

The room, and the patient, had been arranged for an audience. Tension, as hope, was high. The procedure, a transorbital lobotomy, had taken only ten minutes. The guests rose in a congratulatory hum and retired to the adjoining room to soothe their nerves and take refreshment. Eight heavy armless chairs faced the table, each silk-upholstered cushion dimpled and warm from its recent occupant.

The skin around Luci's orbits blackened like spilled ink. She opened her eyes, breaking the dark room with a meteor gaze. The cold metal hardware of the restraints pushed into her wrists and ankles, and she felt the muscles in her legs and arms contract and twist into one continuous knot. A woman appeared at her side and laid a hand on her shoulder.

"Doctor!"

The man who had just taken the ice picks from Luci's brain entered the room and set a glass of whisky on the sideboard next to the instruments, suffusing the air with smoke and splinters.

"There's our patient, awake!" The man shined a light into Luci's eyes. He pressed a stethoscope to her chest under her cotton gown and listened to her heartbeat. He did not undo the straps.

"Capital, capital!" the doctor said to no one. To the nurse he said, "Take her to her rooms, then. Tomorrow we begin the real work, full steam ahead! By God, we've done it. Our Luci will be a brand-new girl!"

As the nurse wheeled the table to the freight elevator at the back of the mansion, Luci closed her eyes and tried to imagine her mother, but instead of the lovely face of Maggie Sykes, there was only a thick blue frost, and the drowning sound of ice cracking against glass.

1 LUCI

Luci Sykes swung her stiletto like a gavel onto the glossy wood until a rind of red patent leather heel peeled off the sole. The mammoth desk revealed not so much as a nick. Luci scowled, and pressed a button on the intercom. "Jasper!"

"Luci. How may I help?" Jasper appeared as cool as an April morning. He glided into the room balancing a cup of jasmine tea on a silver tray, dressed as though suiting up was what he did for a living—tapered leg, cinched waist, English textiles, hand stitched Italian shoes—but dressing was not what Jasper did for a living. Luci was his vocation.

Today she detected an uptick in scrutiny under his suave demeanor. She imagined she warranted some watching. It was not her business to reign herself in, to stem the savage impulses. That was Jasper's job.

"Jasper, what's the word on Lamb?" Less than two weeks earlier, immediately after Luci's mother's death, Olympia's Chief Operations Officer, Theodore Lamb, disappeared with a quantity of critical software. Despite Olympia's resources, or more likely because of them, he was thus far untraceable.

"None yet. The old dog is proving himself pretty nimble. I'm confident, though, we'll have him presently. And BEACON." BEACON, Olympia's penultimate global positioning system, was currently in use in billions of devices across the planet. Theodore Lamb had made off with a proprietary version used to help develop SEARCHLIGHT, Luci's latest creation, set to debut worldwide within the month.

When Luci Sykes applied her energies to a project, dark roads were illuminated and the human species pressed forward. When her electricity went ungrounded, she sputtered like a frayed wire in a puddle. Her significant intellectual skills had thus far created and promoted a global showroom of innovations: revolutionary engine designs, navigational programs, and whole diverse systems for sustainable fuel production. Fired up, Luci could, and did, change the world. Bored, she would just as soon burn it to ash. Jasper tended the coals.

Jasper thought himself a self-made man, a status both accurate and slippery. Certainly, Jasper Collins, Senior Vice-President of Olympia Navigation, was his own meticulous construction, designed to perfectly occupy every nipped inch of his Hugo Boss worsted wool, with no room for memory of when he would not have. Sometimes it was his former self that felt like a construct. Jasper's past was a cinematic tool—a colorful, sordid backstory he never told, and few knew. Luci knew.

They met at the crumbling edge of childhood, and in fifteen years, they'd rarely strayed more than a city block from one another. Jasper presented as the perfect executive assistant, a super-elevated servant to Luci's sovereign, but the truth was more complex.

Their incarnations in the present hierarchy were roles they wore with the plasticity of an eternally bound couple, returning life after life to play it out again.

Luci's suspicions about Jasper's sharpened regard were correct. He had indeed recently observed Luci pushing the boundaries of her known mercury. His gut fluttered and seized, not knowing exactly what was happening with her, when knowing was his purpose. Luci depended on him for it, or did. His prescience was elemental to everything they had achieved in the last decade. Luci provided the wild germinating force, the rocket fuel, the energy of their partnership. He collected it, housed it, and beamed it where it did optimal good, or optimal damage, whichever was called for. Theirs had been an extremely profitable and effective pairing. Currently, however, something was off between them. Jasper could feel that Luci herself didn't yet grasp the breach. This time, she was fired up to launch without him.

"I can't say I share your confidence, Jasper, but I trust you to keep our path clear.

Lamb can stay gone, as long as he stays out of our way."

Jasper appreciated the inclusion. Even so, he twitched slightly as Luci brought her heel down one last time on her reflection in the black wood.

2 TOKKER

Tokker smelled the ions shifting. He cut the engine and rolled the bike into the lilac shading the charcoal ruins of the old work shed. At the back door, a tile from the edge of the eave of the farmhouse succumbed to gravity and hit Tokker on the head. So much for surviving another tornado season intact.

"Esther, I'm home!" Tokker bent to pat the sagging flanks of Hercules, whose massive, thumping tail belied an advanced muscular degeneration. Tokker knew Herc's hearing was still good, though, unlike Esther's. Esther, he was sure, was not yet aware of his presence, despite the shout out.

He took the stairs three at a time. His great aunt sat in her chair in the corner bedroom, rock still except for her eyes, which found him like a drone as he filled the doorway.

"Hey, Esther. What would you say to a turkey pot pie?"

Herc whined from the bottom of the stairs. Tokker had felt OK, at first, leaving Esther in Herc's care while he was at work. The dog could fetch a phone, even nose the emergency button on Esther's wrist. Very lately, though, the old boy struggled with the stairs, and appeared continually distraught, as if he'd been fired, or forcibly retired.

Tokker picked up the tray of cold toast and tea dregs. He'd heat up some dinner before Penelope got there to get Esther ready for bed, and then he'd sit with the pile of bills that had spread like mold on the kitchen table.

The microwave dinged as the doorbell honked. Tokker's first thought was that the machine was blowing up, another broken thing. He breathed a thick "Aw, fuck you" to the appliance.

"That's a bit premature, I think, but I am delighted to make your acquaintance." Tokker pivoted to a figure outside the kitchen screen door. The figure wore a suit under a trench coat, and held a shoebox.

"I hopped back here when no one came round to the front, back doors are friendlier, anyway, don't you agree? May I come in? I'm an old friend of your mother's, since before you were born. I'd like to introduce myself properly." The man looked to the sky, then back to Tokker. "And, you know, I believe we're about to get a bit of weather."

As if on cue, a heavy curtain dropped on the day and the sky cracked open.

Tokker leaned into the screen, allowing the visitor to pass.

"Forgive me, appearing like this with no warning. I am Theodore Lamb, Esq. I am the executor of your mother's estate."

"Listen, Sir, I thank you for coming clear out here, especially with this weather coming on, but I believe you've made a mistake. My mother died some twenty-eight years ago, and left nothing like an 'estate', I can tell you that. Maybe you got the wrong name off the internet. Look, you're welcome to wait out the rain, I got some coffee, a beer if you want, but I'm pretty sure you're in the wrong part of town, Mr...."

"Lamb. Theodore. Thank you. But there's no mistake, Mr. Sykes, or may I call you Tokker? It is most definitely you whom I seek. I have an imperative to apprise you of your position, now that your mother has passed."

"Mr. *Lamb*—Ted—maybe you didn't hear me. My mother died 28 years ago, giving birth to me. And the name's Lindstrom, not Sykes or whatever. You know what, I've changed my mind— you gotta go. I don't have time for crazy today." Tokker grasped the older man's shoulder firmly and attempted to maneuver him toward the door. It was surprisingly difficult.

9

"Tokker, it's perfectly reasonable for you to be incredulous, many people have taken great care to keep you in the dark. But I am legally compelled, by your own mother's decree, to enlighten you now. There is much at stake." Mr. Lamb reached into the inside pocket of his suit jacket as Tokker grasped the screen door handle with his free hand, edging the older man out of the kitchen with the opposite forearm. Lamb extracted a square snapshot, burnt with age at the corners, of a woman and a little girl, five or six years of age. The woman matched exactly the picture of his mother Esther kept on her dresser, minus the child kneeling before her in the sand. Lamb held the image to the young man's face.

Tokker stopped pushing, but continued to clamp Lamb's shoulder as he snatched the photo from the lawyer's fingertips.

"That's my mother!"

"Yes. And the person beside her is your sister, Luci Sykes."

"Who did you say you were?"

"I speak for your mother. Her death makes this meeting possible. I'm so sorry. This must be a terrible shock. But the quicker I can convince you of the urgency of my visit, the quicker you can intervene in what will otherwise be an epic disaster for you and your sister, and, assuredly, for many others. Please, may I sit?"

Tokker released his grip, nodded, and gestured toward a kitchen chair. He noticed, as if for the first time, a laceration in the red vinyl seat, a bit of batting blooming from the split. He stood there, adrift for a moment, wondering if he should get the duct tape. Herc loped over and stuck his wet nose in Tokker's palm, bringing him back. "Hey, boy. Right. Let's get you and Esther some dinner, eh? Mr., um, Lamb, can I get you a beer? Or, what, tea? I'm going to run some dinner upstairs to my aunt, and feed this beast, and then maybe you can explain some of this to me."

3 ESTHER

Esther looked down at the old dog, restless and twitching on the faded hooked rug next to her chair. She hoped he was chasing rabbits. If dogs had nightmares, this one would have plenty of terrible pictures to replay in his sleep. If she could talk, she'd tell him what a good beast he was. Is, poor thing. *The old dog moves scarcely more than I do these days*, she thought. She wondered at her own sentimentality. Esther had always been kind, in her way, but not much for reverie.

Esther's hearing was better than she let on. No point, she reasoned, on insisting upon too much communication. The boy had enough to deal with. *Now it's some kind of visitor downstairs*, she could hear. That was unusual. She could smell the dog food on Herc's breath, which preceded him as he pulled himself up the stairs to sleep under her feet. *He* didn't seem concerned. But a visitor, someone other than the girl, that was not usual. She stiffened in her chair.

Esther had spent a good deal of energy staying alert to things that seemed out of the ordinary, often only to her. She and Jed, her companion of so many years, her partner, her love, built this house, and the life within it, to be perfectly ordinary. Which is to say, un-extraordinary—invisible, even—to protect the boy. Jed was only too happy to retire to this little fiction Esther created, even if she herself had to grow into it. She never, in all those years, let her guard down, but once. That time, it cost her Jed.

She knew the second she felt the involuntary tightening of her muscles, it would be this way, and yet, even knowing, she let time slip away without telling the boy what he needed to know. So foolish, she thought, and here he was now a man, an ignorant man, with a visitor. A fuse of regret and fear snaked like a lit coil through her brain. Her body remained largely unmoved, but for the whitening of her knuckles, and the faint tap of a slippered toe.

4 LAMB LEAVES

Tokker swung a longneck from the index and middle fingers on his left hand. He paced, staring wildly at the dim linoleum, craning his neck in an effort to give the information coming from the old man an easier point of entry. When the story was told, Tokker offered Lamb the couch for the night. It was late, and the wind and the rain had not let up. Lamb refused the hospitality, politely, and insisted on driving back to his hotel, some 50 miles off. By the porch light, through the screen, through the rain, Tokker now noticed the blackest, sleekest, fastest-looking vehicle he'd ever laid eyes on. Lamb turned to Tokker.

"You'll have questions, Tokker. Please, ask them. I have a cell phone expressly for this purpose, your questions. Again, forgive me, forgive this intrusion. If it were just a question of money, this meeting would not have been necessary. Many people need you to know your real story, despite the work of a select few to keep it from you. I would have kept it from you, myself, but that is just an aging gentleman's desire for peace." They shook hands. With his free arm Lamb grasped Tokker where his hairline met his neck and pulled him into a half embrace, resting his own head against the young man's for a moment before quickly assuming his formal posture. "Take care, Tokker. I'll be in touch."

The wind took the screen door as Lamb opened it, slamming it against the house, and yanking the old man's arm with it. "Best batten down the hatches, eh?"

Tokker popped the cap off another beer, ignoring the first one, still half full. The lawyer, or whatever this Mr. Lamb was, had produced and left behind a manila envelope of documents. There was his mother's will and a fair pile of legal documents, in addition to the shoebox of photographs. He added that first picture, the one on the beach of his mother and the little girl, to the pile now scattered across the milky veined Formica of the table. Luci. He had a sister, her name was Luci. There were more pictures of the girl and the woman together, smiling and not, on sailboats and in fancy flower gardens. Some photographs were taken indoors, in big rooms with expensive-looking furniture. Luci looked to be no older than seven or eight in most of them, quite a bit younger in a few.

One photograph diverged from the story laid out in front of him. Luci must have been thirteen, if the date in the upper corner was correct. It would have been impossible to know, otherwise. Her head was shaven, and she was strapped to a table, legs bare, a hospital gown twisted into her torso. She could have been thirteen or thirty. In this one, she is alone.

A headache wormed up from a pinprick at the back edge of Tokker's hairline to the top of his cranium. This morning he had felt half-buried by what he now saw as normal shit— taking care of his sick aunt, watching his dog die, keeping his splintering house whole. This morning felt like a lifetime ago. He tried to get a grip on the facts, as they were given to him. His mother was dead. She was dead when he woke up this morning, but now she was dead in a whole new way. Freshly dead, not yet two weeks dead. Not twenty-eight years dead, like she was this morning. His sister, who was nonexistent this morning, was alive.

There was money, a load of money, the fact of which would be interesting if he weren't so completely buffaloed by the rest of the information. All these people suddenly connected to him, and some of them unstable, even dangerous. He couldn't imagine why any of them would care about him. He fixed engines, lived on the outskirts of nowhere in a tumble-down house soon to be blown away by a little wind and rain. He didn't even own a computer, just used the one in town at the library to write invoices and send a few emails, poached off the diner's internet with his flip phone for anything else. He mentioned this to Lamb, wondering how exactly he managed to find him, anyway.

It was hard to hear that Lamb, and his mother, knew where he was the whole time. These past few months especially, struggling to make ends meet, now with Jed gone, and taking care of Esther, he'd never felt more lonesome. Now just like that, he was supposed to step up, into a mess made by a bunch of strangers? Because of so-called blood? "Bullshit," he said out loud, and swigged his beer.

Tokker mistook the high-pitched sound for a ringing in his ears, before he realized it was Herc, baying from Esther's room upstairs. *Esther!* Penelope never showed up, he realized, probably decided not to make the trip in the storm. *Shit, shit, shit. At least the dog's got his priorities straight,* he thought. Esther was alive and real and upstairs waiting for someone to help her get to bed, had been waiting with the light on for hours. *Goddammit,* he thought, *pull yourself together, asshole. Alfred shows up in the Batmobile with a plot to save Gotham, and you let everything go to hell.* He climbed the stairs.

5 LAMB IS RESOLVED

Lamb wasn't worried about the storm. The vehicle was impervious to almost every external force, be it nature, bullets, or his own incompetence. He drove it, nominally, but it was programmed to intuit anything less than optimal maneuvering, in which case it overrode manual application and drove itself. Driving for Lamb was, at this point, a vanity.

The young man had been shocked, of course, and reasonably so. It would have been a kindness to leave him be, leave him to his ordinary troubles. Kindness wasn't a commodity in this family, though. Lamb sped past the hotel, and programmed a new course. He was too tired for the pretense. Apprising Tokker of his situation strenuously taxed both body and brain; it was almost too much to bear to know that Esther was in that porous wreck of a house somewhere. Esther—fitting enough, that name, though not the one Lamb had known her by long ago. *Oh, to be so near!* Lamb tasted the metallic bitterness of once again subverting desire for duty.

In the moment when he considered reprogramming the route and heading back to the farmhouse, the bloodless vehicle, as if sensing a sea change, announced, *Course set.*

6 LUCI & THE WORD

Luci touched a spot on the beveled edge of the table and a holographic screen came to life mid-room. The image revealed a view of the latest version of her global positioning software, SEARCHLIGHT, soon to be adopted by corporations and governments worldwide. This was the future, visible and suspended for a few final days in her office. She recited under her breath, "In the beginning was the Word, and the Word was with God, and the Word was God..." *No*, she thought, *it wasn't any goddamn word that came first. It wasn't some reckless thing ill formed and half understood.*

No: in the beginning there was light.

Then came the nothing, and then the fire. Searing, cauterizing, fire. After, after, came the word, the words—endless tangles of words, words stuck in your teeth, clogging your ears, lodged in your throat, binding your wrists, lost, lost in your brain. Words to lure you in to dark places, words to still you.

Luci did not herself speak until she was sixteen. In her oldest memory, generated, she believed, in utero, she recognized the sound of her mother's voice, but distinguished no specific language, no words. Instead she experienced the sound of her mother as positioning, as place.

After the lobotomy and the therapies, Luci could speak. She developed a voice, and with it an extraordinary vocabulary. She developed, as well, according to her medical team and anyone who spoke with her, an unprecedented grasp of the nuances of speech. In a single year after she began to speak, Luci could converse fluently in all the romance languages, as well as Arabic, Russian, Farsi, Japanese, Mandarin, Hindi, several Inuit dialects—any language introduced to her, in fact.

It seemed all Luci had to do was converse with a native speaker for an afternoon, and she learned not only the rudiments, but the subtleties of a tongue, as well. It was an extraordinary gift, not one that was anticipated. The men who came to the institute to speak with Luci sometimes left weeping, moved by the way teenaged Luci's grasp of their native tongue recalled a grandmother or a whole, lost village.

Jasper and Luci met somewhere during this burst of loquaciousness. He, too, felt weirdly understood by Luci, seen in a way that made him feel stripped.

Unlike the medical team and various so-called experts, Jasper never confused Luci's acumen with wisdom. He had no ancestors to resurrect, no generational thread, no stories, no village. Jasper was not amazed so much by what Luci said, as by how she held her body as she said it. He saw her genius, yes, but he immediately recognized Luci's skills as a bit of brilliant wiring, precariously housed in an undernourished and feral frame.

He did not ascribe companion feelings such as compassion and empathy to Luci's *gift*, as the team was fond of calling it. There was something dangerous in the way she accepted their praise. She bowed her head, fingers entwined, the shy supplicant, seemingly overcome with gratitude and humility as they marveled and gushed. They trusted her modesty. They owned her, had earned her; she was their just desserts for their applied acuity, their tireless efforts. Jasper sometimes felt as though he was the only one really looking at her. To him, she presented as something barely contained. She vibrated. Her downward gaze burned a hole under their feet. After, and always, her silence roared in his brain.

Jasper stood in the doorway, watching Luci watch her creation.

"The word, Jasper, the word. I believe I have chosen well, at last. The bloody word may or may not have started it all, but it sure as hell is going to end it."

18

7 TOKKER LEAVES

When Tokker woke up the morning after Lamb's visit, the pain in his head was gone, replaced by a strange vibration in or around his ear, not a ringing, exactly, but a taut cord of energy. A half-empty beer bottle attested to the unlikelihood of a hangover, unless it was an information hangover that was giving him the shakes.

Papers and photographs strewed the table. So he hadn't been dreaming. "Jesus," Tokker said aloud, "this *can't* be real." Hercules shuffled in with a low wag. "Well, boy, looks like we got ourselves another day. I think this one might get a little weird."

Penelope appeared at the kitchen door, which meant it was around seven o'clock.

"Mornin' there, Sport. I'd say you've looked better."

Tokker muttered a "Mornin'," and quickly shuffled the papers on the table together into a pile. "Didn't get much sleep."

"Well, maybe you shouldn't spend every night worrying over a stack of bills. There's always gonna be bills, you know. Can't make yourself sick over it."

Tokker nodded, and got busy making a pot of coffee while Penelope went to see about getting Esther out of bed. He put the kettle on to boil, scrambled a half dozen eggs, and dumped two thirds of them into Hercules' dish. He brought a cup of tea, a piece of marmalade toast, and the remainder of the eggs on a tray up to his aunt. He heard Penelope and Esther moving around in the hall bathroom, Penelope's warm and musical voice holding up the conversation for the both of them. He set the tray on the dresser, and glanced at the photograph of his mother, young and smiling, next to a squinting Esther, buttoned up in an overcoat and brimmed hat, on a boardwalk. Atlantic City? Coney Island? Canada? He wondered at his own lack of curiosity all these years.

He went downstairs and took the envelope and the documents into the parlor. Tokker rarely used this room, or even entered it. Esther used to spend a lot of time in here, reading, mostly. It seemed like a neutral place to try to sort some of this out. His mother's death certificate was dated 12 days prior. A medical record stated,

Deceased: Margaret Annabelle Preston-Sykes. Cause of death: Asphyxiation. Asphyxiation? Tokker wondered what the hell that meant. Was it an accident? A suicide? His mother had been dead to him for so long, he couldn't organize his brain and heart well enough to decide what it was he felt about her actual death, let alone understand how it occurred. His awareness in the moment could not extend much beyond his own general, whole-body ache.

Tokker felt pulled upon and weak. The enormous disconnect between the circumstances of his mother's life and his own opened a dangerous gap in his understanding of the universe. Never in his days would he have imagined himself the son of an heiress. Esther and Jed had done OK, built this house, clothed and fed him well enough as he grew. He hadn't known any real want, even managed a couple of years of college before times got tougher and he went to work full time at the shop. Like lots of other places, the town hadn't fared so well in the last decade or so. It's true there wasn't a ton of regular engine work, but they'd managed all right, at least until this last stretch, with Jed dying in that accident, and then, when Esther took sick.

But his mother, it appeared, was to the manor born. That's how rich people were described on those programs Esther used to like to watch on the public television channel, when the antenna worked. Boat races, horses paddocked in barns bigger and better than the house he stood in, more bathrooms than you could count, a live-in staff come a-running whenever. That had been his mother's reality, and, he assumed, his twin sister's. *And the lawyer! What the hell was with the frigging spaceship the old geezer took off in?* Tokker resented his sudden resentment, and felt overcome with a ridiculous nostalgia for his poverty. Doubly ridiculous, he thought, as he remained, at that moment, poor—Alfred, Lamb, whoever that guy was—failed to mention any immediate change in his financial status. *He sure as shit didn't show up at the kitchen door with a gigantic goddamn Publishers Clearinghouse check,* Tokker thought. Instead, Lamb had brought plenty of bad news: a dead again mother, a resurrected and dangerous sister, and a plot. *Just like TV.*

With the wind gone, the warped panes were quiet in their frames. Bright morning sun illuminated old Herc like the baby Jesus on the rug in front of the window. Too bad, Tokker thought: this might've been the perfect time to be taken by a tornado, Emerald City or no.

The low hum in Tokker's ear turned to static, which became a voice, or something like a voice, something he understood.

Mr. Sykes, please speak with Penelope about taking care of Esther today. Proper arrangements for her care will be made shortly. Get to the post office. There's a key for a postal box under your doormat. Waste no time, please.

For a long moment, Tokker questioned his sanity. Frightened, he raced through the house and up the stairs to Esther's room. Penelope and she were sitting in front of the window, bathed in the same light that had lit Herc. Penelope was laughing lightly through some local gossip, helping Esther take a bite of egg. Esther's eyes met Tokker's the moment he reached the doorway, panting. And he knew. He knew in that moment, absolutely, that Esther, his petrified, speechless great aunt had a great deal to tell him.

"Penelope. Esther and I need a big favor. Could you please stick around today? I can pay you, I promise. It's last minute, I know, but I wouldn't ask if it wasn't an emergency. I've got to take care of some stuff right away, it can't wait. Can you do it?"

"Well, yeah, I think it'd be all right. I gotta call Charlie, let him know he's got to get the kids off to school, pick 'em up and all. But sure, I can do it. You gonna be OK?

"Um, I'm not sure, Pen. But hey, no, yes, I'm fine, it's gonna be fine. I just have to take off today to set a few things straight, then we'll be good. I sure do appreciate it, Pen, I mean it. Hey, I think I'll sit here and talk with Esther for a minute or two, if you want to call home."

"Yeah, Tokker, sure. I'll go call Charlie, and be right back. Esther and me'll have a real girls' day in, huh? Or maybe hit the casino, who knows?" She winked at Esther and patted Tokker's arm on the way out of the room, but the crease between her eyes deepened as she descended the stairs. Penelope was a woman who knew when something had hit the fan.

"Esther," Tokker began, "I've got a strong feeling there's things you would tell me if you could, things that maybe you should've told me a lot sooner." Esther felt something slip inside. Since the moment she became his guardian, Esther would willingly have thrown her body between this boy, this man, and any threat to his safety. Now, when he truly needed her, her body was stone still, worthless. She couldn't even talk to him.

Esther locked her gaze on Tokker, willing him to grasp her intention. They held each other that way for some time before Esther slowly moved her gaze in the direction of the dresser, drawing Tokker's attention to the photograph. He reached for it. Her eyes returned to him, then, and remained on him, unblinking.

The static crackled again, and Tokker heard, *Please, Mr. Sykes.* Adrenaline coursed through his system, contracting his muscles, his stomach, his bowels. *Oh, God,* he thought, *I'm doing this—God knows where to do God knows what—but I'm really doing this.* Tokker bent to kiss Esther on her forehead, and as he did, she jerked her head to face the dresser.

"I love you, Esther." He grabbed the image and was gone.

8 LAMB & MAGGIE

Lamb regretted this course of action with the young man, but Lamb regretted a lot of things, and regret never seemed to bear much impact on his actions. The terms of Maggie's will were explicit, if bizarre. Tokker was sent to live with Esther so that he could grow into manhood uncontaminated by the Sykes miasma, and unharmed by Abner Ruggles, his natural father. He was to be reared in the *real world*, so as to develop an immunity from the fetid, seething parasitic organism that was his blood family. Maggie believed that this was the only way to save both her children: one day her children would be reunited, and Tokker would be the antibody to their cancer, the balm to Luci's suffering.

It was ludicrous, Lamb was sure. Maggie was so often addled by a complex cocktail of Placidyl, Seconal, Dalmane, Librium, and various other sedatives, it was hard to tell fervor from fantasy. Margaret Preston-Sykes didn't present delusional, though.

While he was privy to her desperation, and several well-compensated physicians were aware of her drug repertoire, she held herself impeccably. Also, she lived a quiet, unsociable life. Of necessity, of course, but he thought she would've chosen it in any case. Maggie's halcyon debutante years had lost their buoyancy, sunk deep in her consciousness long ago.

Lamb's memory remained vivid. It was plain early on that Maggie had inherited her father's, Emanuel Sykes', joie de vivre, and at seventeen, bore her mantle as an American heiress with devastating grace. She was beautiful, as young wealthy people are beautiful, but her effect had more to do with her ability to hone her attention. In possession of all her father's gifts, she could reject his vanity, and take strength not from how she was seen by the world, but by how she

23

recognized herself in it. Maggie's genuine interest in the human experience made her a natural ambassador and executor of her father's philanthropy. Public health led the list, primarily child welfare, but as Maggie came into adulthood, private money in their circles went with increased concentration toward progressive treatments for mental illness. Nineteenth century urban asylums underwent vast remodels; modern facilities went up in the farmlands of New Jersey and Long Island. Research was funded. At gala benefits, Maggie seemed to engage every politician, scientist, industry baron, and society matron in conversation well beyond the usual party patter. Everyone was made to feel unique and entirely essential in their role. Everyone mattered. Maggie gave the impression that one's absence would critically disable the great work that was underway, while one's presence all but guaranteed its triumph.

At nineteen Maggie met a young scientist who worked in research and development at a growing pharmaceutical company. Their romance kindled on a shared idealism, and blazed on their mutual exquisiteness. The bright scientist, however, would occasionally go dark, retreat into periods of moodiness that increased, in their time together, in both duration and frequency. In a shining moment they were married. In a subsequent eclipse she found him pale and lifeless in their bathroom, the paraphernalia of his self-treatment wagging from the crook of a naked elbow.

Maggie entertained no other romance until Abner Ruggles presented himself almost five years later. Emanuel Sykes disliked him immediately, but Lamb could see that despite his distaste, the patriarch welcomed the re-animation of his daughter. Sykes had liked the other boy, so handsome and well mannered. Ruggles came from coarse stuff, that much was clear. Emanuel Sykes was not naive, nor did he build castles around his own path to prosperity. Grit was important, moreso these days, he felt, and Ruggles had grit. If he did not exude the kindness he would have wanted for his child, well, perhaps she would bring it out in him. Lamb never shared what he'd heard in other, shadowed circles about Abner Ruggles' rough rise through the social strata, not with Emanuel, not with Maggie. No one was left to absolve him of that particular sin of omission.

Lamb had been vociferous, however, in his opinions regarding Maggie's scheme to reunite her children. It was plainly insane to him to think that a young man raised in virtual poverty, with limited education, and only perhaps a small affinity for the mechanical, could right this Titanic of a family, let alone affect the machinations of global development, or have any effect whatsoever on a force of nature like Luci Sykes. In his protests, he did not mention Esther, or what it would mean to bring her back into the picture. Lamb had kept quiet about his attachment there, and anyway, like her father before her, Maggie dismissed any thought that Lamb might have loyalties or passions unrelating to them. Beyond his personal feelings, however, he had no doubt that poking the hive would arouse the ire and retribution of Queen Esther.

Regardless, it was a moot point. The young man was on his way. The chip he'd planted behind Tokker's dusty ear last night had spoken, and the boy had listened. He would go to the post office, use the key Lamb left to open up a box, and leave everything he knew behind.

Tokker was confused. Inside the postal box was an old flip phone, much like his own piece of crap. No note, no map, no self-destructing tape recorder, no gun, no cyanide pill. *What the hell?* He considered that the thing probably wouldn't even work, given the shitty service out here in God's country. A sticky tab on the back of the plastic casing said, "Go to the bathroom." *Yeah, real James Bond stuff,* he thought.

The bathroom was a one-hole closet out the side door to the left of the postal boxes. Tokker went in, latched the door, ridiculously, pulled the chain for the single bare light bulb, and wondered what had crawled in there and died. *Jesus, what a stink.*

Then he flipped open the phone. Another tab: "Press 411."

As his finger released its pressure from the keypad, a series of translucent blue and green beams appeared before Tokker and organized themselves into a grid. Something like sound, but not, filled his body.

Hello, Mr. Sykes. I am BEACON, a positioning service

25

programmed to guide you on your forthcoming journey. You may speak, or you may simply think. I will comprehend and respond accordingly.

"Holy shit!" Tokker sat down on the toilet, and let the phone fall from his hand.

Mr. Sykes, I comprehend that you have experienced something of an information overload, and that my technology is shocking your system. Please take a moment to refresh.

Tokker took a breath, regretted it, and picked up the phone, but couldn't decide what to do. *Speak to it?*

Technically, the plastic device will be necessary until we get ourselves properly synced, Mr. Sykes, but you needn't speak directly to it.

"Tokker, if you don't mind." Then he thought, *Are you a you?*

I'm sorry, Tokker. If my manner of addressing you is incorrect, Tokker, you may make changes to my settings.

"Tell you the truth, uh, *BEACON*, any manner you address me is guaranteed to freak me out at the moment. But just for fun, what settings are we talking about?"

Tokker, my interface is highly programmable. You can select a gendered or nongender specific timbre, language, dialect or accent. I can sound virtually however you want me to sound. For example, you may choose female north Atlantic, female mid Atlantic, female Gulf Coast, female American south, male American mid-west, male southern California, gender neutral Cascadia...

"Well, that's really something..."

...accented English inspired by Puerto Rico, all countries of Central and South America, Caribbean, Continental, German, Italian, Russian, a full Celtic repertoire, West and South African...

"Ok, BEACON, I get it. You do voices. Lemme ask you

something—you got one you like best?

I'm sorry, Tokker, My software is not designed to accommodate a preference singular to itself.

"You sure? I feel like you're doing all the heavy lifting here, and having none of the fun."

Tokker, I am not able to lift anything, but if you were to insist that I accommodate a preference, I might manage a Scottish brogue.

"Ooh, strong choice, there, Bea! Can I call you Bea? If you're going to be buzzing in my ear and God knows where, we might as well drop the formalities. Unless I am losing my mind, then it doesn't matter anyway. Let's assume this shit is real and happening, and you and I agree to be friendly. Whaddya say, Bea?"

Aye, Tokker.

"That's it, Bea, nice and easy. Now, the plan can't be to hide out in the shitter all day. What do you got lined up for us?"

No, Tokker, it is not the plan to stay in this location. Please exit the shitter. Your vehicle has arrived and is ready to take you to your next destination.

"Take *us*, right, Bea? And Jesus, watch your language, will you?"

9 LUCI & SEARCHLIGHT

Nothing was perfect. Or, to be more precise, Luci thought, one rarely saw the perfection of a thing. It could be that her latest positioning system, SEARCHLIGHT, was already perfect, and she just didn't see it. To Luci's eye, several flaws marred her creation's virtue. The wheels of commerce were in motion, however, and she had very little time to cross her t's and dot her i's. In a mere few weeks, she, Luci Sykes, aka, Olympia Navigation, would release SEARCHLIGHT into the world, to live in vehicles and devices virtually everywhere, replacing systems that would seem like toys by comparison. For Luci's master plan to have the effect she desired, it had to roll out on time, lay any comparable tool to waste immediately. Luci was recognized for her ambition, her ability to set lofty goals and exceed them, to turn out products few other tech companies dreamed of, let alone manufactured. Some industry pundits wondered why Olympia was producing a new navigation system so close on the heels of the wildly popular BEACON, which had been operating brilliantly, to great reviews, for less than two years. BEACON was intuitive, encyclopedic, endlessly responsive. Users claimed that operating with BEACON was like having an omniscient yet submissive being by your side, able to anticipate an itch before it was even a tickle. Critics said, sourly, that it was probable that Olympia Navigation had peaked, was going back to an overdrawn well, had nothing truly new to offer with this new system. Some scoffed the new release was just something to keep the tech junkies happy—a dry, meatless, albeit expensive bone to pick over until Olympia could produce an authentically original device.

Luci understood the importance of coming in strong, the impact of dazzle. It was true that SEARCHLIGHT was making its debut before the party for BEACON completely died down. She intended to create a keener sense of urgency with the short turnaround, to give the new launch a breathlessness that could only be the result of an enormous leap forward in the tech. Truthfully, she didn't have much faith in her assessment of the market. It didn't matter. SEARCHLIGHT was no ploy: the system eclipsed everything else, including BEACON. Luci's creation effactually imbued the user with the power of telekinesis. No one had yet seen anything like it. Users would be falling over themselves to make the switch, she had no doubt. It would be the standard, utterly ubiquitous. It would become unthinkable to operate in the world without it.

In much of the world, anyway, and that was one of its flaws. It was a simple matter to get SEARCHLIGHT into most corners of the planet via personal vehicles, cell phones, or through any military operation with any kind of presence in suffering pockets across the globe. There were isolated populations, however small and remote, that could conceivably do without SEARCHLIGHT. Luci weighed her determination to canvass the earth with her creation against the fertile possibilities of a few tiny sub cultures. Well, she reasoned, if the human animal was that hell-bent on survival, it could try its luck with some peaceful reindeer shepherds or Himalayan monks. Or whoever eluded the system's reach and was left functioning and intact on the three-month anniversary of SEARCHLIGHT's release. Every other male who asked SEARCHLIGHT for directions or used it to position a missile would be rendered sterile within twelve weeks, if not sooner. Luci took great care to be the sole owner of that information. Design and production were segmented in such a way that no one person other than Luci understood exactly how all the pieces fit together, let alone what the puzzle was really for. Olympia's engineers and staff were accustomed to secrecy, even amongst themselves. The plan had been hardest to keep from Jasper, who often read her mind without the benefit of supplemental technology.

The other significant problem with SEARCHLIGHT had nothing to do with the system itself, but with the company. The profits from sales of SEARCHLIGHT were projected to be astronomical. Luci had long since stopped caring about how much money the company made, had never cared very much so long as she had the resources to create and produce. The problem was the other major party in line to benefit so obscenely from her work. Thus far Luci had been unable to manipulate or negotiate Abner Ruggles out of Olympia Navigation, and it stoked the kind of frustration she knew when she was very small—a deaf and sightless rage. Luci actually attempted to sell SEARCHLIGHT to a competitor, with the stipulation that she retain control over its development, but no other company had the talent and resources to take it on, which meant her dear father would stand to gain, again, from her achievement.

Luci opened a drawer at her desk, took out a long lighter and a can of Aqua Net hairspray, depressed the nozzle, and pulled the trigger on the lighter. A spray of flame reached nearly to the paneled door.

"That will be a nice touch of drama for your next career charming the cash out of pyromaniac boys at the Midway." Jasper felt his eyebrows warm. "I can see you are deep in thought. You should know we've picked up some activity on Lamb."

"Well," said Luci. She lit up another stream, and contemplated the blaze. "Maybe one problem's going to get fixed before launch, after all."

10 MAGGIE & LUCI

Maggie never thought to abandon her daughter. Not when she understood that delaying Luci's birth had stemmed the oxygen to her brain, or when Luci lagged weeks and months behind the developmental milestones that other children (that Luci's brother, Maggie knew) sailed past, or even when Luci flopped and foamed on the floor, overcome with rage and frustration. Maggie's loyalty to her daughter grew only more vehement in those moments. Luci lacked conformity, but the child had fire. Intensity. And she had a fierce ability to focus. At three years old, she could spend an entire morning in the garden, studying insects, a single insect, could tell which bird belonged to which song, loved to lie on her back for hours under the night sky, arms and legs spread wide, taking in the stars. Maggie had loved Luci, certainly, as someone both belonging to her and also as an entity far beyond her. She cared for her as one would a divine oracle with whom one was entrusted, with a kind of worship. The child had been her light, her inspiration, her invitation to grace.

Maggie had often asked herself how could she have let that beautiful child be taken from her. She would never reconcile it. She tried, at different stages, to blame it on the drugs, or on her husband. She saw the logic of external events. But she'd done it before, hadn't she, given up a child? Both times she told herself it was for the good of the child, but her gut burned with the knowledge that it only held true for Tokker, her son.

She'd let go of Luci. She did not protect her daughter. For her, it was that simple.

Maggie's husband and Luci's father, Abner Ruggles, was moved, as well, by his daughter, but far differently. The child unsettled him. To Ruggles, Luci had been an unnervingly silent baby and a distinctly inanimate toddler, except when she was throwing one of her fits. He thought she might have been a pretty thing, if she weren't so distracted. The child ignored him, except for the occasional level stare. In her glare he was shamed, somehow, and angered.

As Luci outgrew some of the violence of her early childhood, she came into her own. While not talkative like other six and seven-year-olds, she liked being around other kids and laughed often, more out of the joy of their company than through a keen understanding of playground humor. Her father retained a speech therapist and a tutor to supplement her elementary studies. While he hadn't quite warmed to Luci, Ruggles appreciated any sign of social blossoming in his daughter. Certainly, she would not be the debutante he'd imagined. She could, though, quite feasibly, eventually, marry someone decent—no up and coming junior Senator, maybe—but a respectable sort, someone useful. Still, he thought it a damn shame that the child turned out the way she did, with a mother as beautiful and sharp as Maggie. He'd come to suspect something wrong in the lineage, there, but Christ, who could've guessed? Maggie Sykes was a magnificent woman, breathtaking! A goddess, and brilliant—spoke French like a native, read everything. Read too much. Read in bed, *bah to that*, he thought. Then there was the money, old and plentiful. When they'd met, he assumed the first husband must have been mad to leave her as he did, to abandon that life, but later he wondered.

At eleven, Luci's child body seemed to process an entire puberty's worth of hormones overnight. Suddenly, breasts and hips. Luci's behavior displayed no great change. She continued to roam the fields beyond the estate, studying beetles and spiders and butterflies. By the time she was thirteen, however, many of the local boys, and several men, were circling like turkey vultures. More than once, one of the servants had gone out looking for Luci, only to find her sitting in the tall grass with some slavering local lothario holding her hand in his lap. Ruggles was horrified that his daughter should be attracting males like a bitch in heat. He would have liked to have had an actual castle so he could lock her in a nice, impenetrable tower. Instead, he sent Luci to a convent school in Wisconsin.

That might have been the end of the problem, as Ruggles saw

32

it. The nuns ran a tight ship, kept beautiful gardens that needed constant tending, and had no problem with Luci being slow in spots. Luci could wait out the awkward years and still come out to society by the time she was eighteen, virginity intact. That was Ruggles' plan, and it would have been fine, he thought, but for that bastard priest. Ruggles still wished he'd made the man suffer more than he did. *Fucker ruined her for anything.*

After that, none of it was any good. The nuns complained that Luci broke the quiet of every night with her screams. She fell into seizures throughout the day, refused to bathe, bit the sisters when they tried to subdue her. Ruggles concluded that there was nothing to do but lock her away. He couldn't bring her back to her mother. Wouldn't, no matter how Maggie begged. Luci was a wild animal, a beast. It was just timing and dumb luck that those doctors saw her when they did, and suggested the treatment. She was just the right age, they said. They could relieve her of the effects of the trauma, both her birth trauma, they said, and the other unfortunate, more recent event. She could be remade, come out a brand-new girl.

And goddamn if she didn't, he thought, though it was years since he actually saw her in person again after he admitted her to Westhaven. He agreed to five years, and signed a waiver releasing the team of responsibility. Told his wife it was the child's best hope for a regular, happy life. He was wrong on that one. There was nothing regular about Luci Sykes (who insisted on her mother's name, once she could speak). When she stepped out of the Institute, her irregularities had all been transformed. As for happiness, Ruggles thought, well, who can say? The slow-witted child had been happy. Maybe in this bloodline, he thought, brilliant and happy just don't know how to live together. Like powerful and happy, maybe it's fundamentally beside the point. Happy doesn't make things happen.

Ambition, now there's a trait. He had to admit, Luci had what it took in that capacity. At this point, he owed everything—his business, his reputation—to his daughter, even if the little bitch had disdained his name. He had to admire her fire. She was terrible, and, in the end, magnificent. Nothing like her mother, of course, but yes, spectacular in her way. She'd turned a profit, and then some. Which didn't mean he was going to lie down and die and hand it all over for a measly monthly check. Oh, no, he'd destroy her, once this next thing was out. Better her than me, he thought, as he knew she'd have his balls if she could.

11 TOKKER & BEA

I'm sorry, Tokker, I don't understand.

"Listen, Bea, you've really got to stop apologizing so much. It's starting to come across as a bad habit, you know, or a glitch. What have you got to be so sorry for all the time?"

I'm sor...Tokker, you are correct in discerning that I am not sorry. It is not a glitch, as you suggest. I am programmed to be submissive. It is intended to disarm bad humor, to soothe.

"Well, I for one do not find it soothing for you to tell me you're sorry every time you talk to me. Or fill up my head, or whatever it is you are doing. In fact, it is the opposite of soothing. It is very irritating, and makes me angry. I already feel stupid and out of my league with all this stuff. Your saying sorry all the time just makes me feel like an asshole, too."

Tokker, you are not stupid or out of a league. If you would permit me, I would like to apologize one more time for making you feel like an asshole.

"Jesus, Bea. It's fine."

Then I may apologize?

"Oh, for Christ's sake! Yes, sure. One last time, and then please, please be done."

Thank you. Tokker, I am sorry you feel like an asshole.

"Thanks, Bea. Better."

When the vehicle pulled up around the back of the post office, Tokker assumed Lamb had returned to get him, although he did wonder why they couldn't have just left together from the house, and dispensed with all the secret key stuff. When the driver side door opened, however, the seat was empty.

Now Tokker and BEACON were speeding northeast on the interstate, with no one at the wheel. In fact, there was no wheel. Tokker sunk down in a seat that molded around his body. There was a control panel in front of him where a dash should have been, but he certainly was not the one controlling anything. Tokker felt like an unconvincing mix of Simon Temple and one of those *Dukes of Hazard* guys.

Tokker, please make yourself comfortable. You will arrive at your destination in approximately three point two five hours.

It was a good hour before Tokker could operate past the terror he felt at being hauled driverless across the country at 120 miles per hour, or could form a mental sequence other than the fiery crash that played out on a loop in his imagination. When he had his brain back, he wondered why he was the guy these people wanted for their mission, or whatever this was. And why did Esther want him to go? What did she know that she couldn't tell him? Esther had always been straight with him about important things, had always looked after him. Now he was given to believe she did more than just bring him up, that she and Jed had been protecting him from something. The next question was, why was she encouraging him to face that something, or someone, now?

Tokker's brain thumped against his skull. It occurred to him that he'd done more talking and listening in the past twelve hours than in any given week of his life. He was grateful Bea had left him to his own thoughts for a bit. He wondered if he could turn her off, or if not, who could. He fell asleep.

12 LAMB REMEMBERS MAGGIE & LUCI

So far, so lucky, thought Lamb. He knew Bea would perfectly navigate the vehicle to the warehouse, but he was less sure of his camouflaging skills. They didn't have to worry about the local police or sheriff's department, of course—never-brought-to-market software enabled the vehicle to speed through any landscape undetected.

Undetected, that is, by law enforcement, who had none of the technology it would have taken to track the vehicle, let alone pull it over. The system knew the location of the authorities long before its own position could be compromised. No, he wasn't worried about the cops. Olympia Navigation didn't just have the tech, they created it. *She* created it. It was only a matter of time before she employed BEACON's successor to pinpoint exactly where they were. Lamb needed time to fill in the gaps for Tokker, and to make him see the importance of disarming Luci before she did something that couldn't be undone.

Not that Lamb couldn't see things from Luci's perspective. In a real way, Luci was more than damaged the day they took her from Maggie, she was murdered.

Something essential died in both of them. Lamb remembered Maggie and Luci in the gardens when Luci was little, identifying the bellflower and hyssop, considering a dragonfly. Luci sought out the bees, injected her face into the pistils of a bloom while a honeybee collected its pollen. Mother and daughter spent hours in the library, Luci on the rug, head bent, legs stretched out in front, enormous copy of *Peterson's Illustrated Guide to Insects* pressed on dimpled knees, Maggie deep in a French novel or a tome on entomology, to keep pace with her child's passion.

Lamb had been struck by their absolute harmony. Certainly the environment was not at all times harmonious. Young Luci suffered prolonged tantrums nearly daily, after which she was often bruised or otherwise injured. Maggie exhibited endless patience with these fits, waiting them out, holding Luci close for hours after they ended, protecting and supporting the child as best she could. For Maggie, these violent spells were an organic piece of Luci, as elemental as her eye color or left-handedness. A forcefully delayed birth had deprived Luci of oxygen, incurring damage to the brain. It was not a consequence of natural forces, it was not God, it was not karma that had affected Luci's development—it was human error. Someone was to blame. Maggie, however, chose to accept the circumstances of her daughter's birth as part of Luci's unique map. Nature or negligence, it did not matter to Maggie, for whom Luci was as perfect as any creature who lived and died. As Maggie's confidante, Lamb knew Maggie didn't just accept Luci's violence.

There was something about the rages that made sense to Maggie. To her they held the power of ritual, catharsis, even powerful criticism. Maggie did not stand apart from Luci's fury, but stood close enough to feel herself implicated in the violence. Often she was humbled by Luci's intensity. There was greatness in it, and vision.

Luci's father, of course, did not share his wife's view of Luci's behavior, let alone her reverence for it. Before the toddler had grown to child, he had a section of the pantry enclosed, padded the walls, and installed a door that locked from the outside. If he was at home when a tantrum came upon Luci, he cornered her and dragged her to the room where she would throw herself against the upholstered walls until she exhausted her rage. When he was away from home, which was often, he left instructions for household staff to do the same, upon penalty of unemployment. No one complied, but neither did anyone ever confront Abner Ruggles, nor question his methods. Except Maggie, of course, who raged, herself, against her husband's deaf barbarism, then begged, then wept, frantic for Luci's release.

Ruggles did not pay much attention to Luci, other than to apply his brand of discipline to her during a tantrum. His wife's and Luci's interests, their quiet absorption, bored him.

He spent most of his time in other haunts. Lamb noted how Ruggles enjoyed attending large public events with his eloquent, elegant wife, liked seeing himself with her by his side in the local media. However, even when he was in town for a big benefit or some such, he more often than not took a suite at his downtown club. When the family left the city for their beach home several weekends a summer, Ruggles spent his days on the boat pretending to fish, and his evenings sipping whisky sours, casting his nets at the yacht club.

Lamb was witness to all of it, drawn in, admittedly, by the sweeping spectacle of wealth and power, but no less by Maggie, in the beginning when she shone alone, and later, when he was compelled by the singular sweetness of the world she spun around herself and Luci. He had initially taken her marriage at face value—glamorous young socialite, handsome brash entrepreneur, a pair for the society pages—but he grew more perplexed by their union the closer he scrutinized it. Why did she accept his violence? After all, the money was hers.

Well, money isn't everything, so they say. Lamb had been around rich people long enough to understand how money, its excesses, could poison the well. Were all rich people unhappy? That seemed too facile. *It's not the money*, Lamb thought. *It's the people.*

Lamb and Luci shared a misanthropic philosophy, clearly. Luci, however, bore more than a simple pessimism for mankind. Luci carried a hatred that threw itself against the walls just as she had thrown herself against the walls of the pantry as a child, only her hatred never exhausted itself. It nourished itself on the fecund production of Luci's spectacularly manufactured brain. Luci was hatred in motion, gaining momentum. And she was looking for him, although Lamb had good reason to believe she wasn't yet aware of how much he knew about her plan to extinguish the possibility of future generations through mass sterilization of the male human species. BEACON, certainly, was not to have shared that. Suddenly (inanely, he thought), he felt sad that he'd never had a child, though as a young man, or a middle-aged one, he'd never wanted one. *We are idiots*, he

39

thought, *always wanting what we can't have, and don't truly desire.*

Lamb felt a pulse in his ear, indicating the vehicle was within a mile of the warehouse. He pulled on his suit jacket and took the elevator up to ground level.

13 THE GARAGE

A circular vulcanized rubber deck cupped the garage, a steel tower oriented by a set of triple-paned glass doors. Identical columns of windows perforated the tower. The vehicle stopped on a platform in front of the deck.

Tokker, you have arrived at your destination. Please exit the vehicle, Bea said.

As Tokker got out, he wondered exactly what city people meant by "garage." The structure was as sleek as any high rise he'd seen in the movies, or in St. Louis, the one time he went with Jed. As he stood there, the vehicle vanished to the back of the building via belted valet.

"Say, Bea, is this home, sweet, home?"

Bea did not respond, but Tokker heard a familiar voice say, "Well, it's not much, but I guess it will do." The glass doors had opened, revealing Theodore Lamb, natty though clearly flagging in a freshly starched shirt.

"You've looked better, Lamb, and I've only met you the one time." Tokker stepped into the tower. The interior was lined entirely in a pattern of spiky rubber.

"You, on the other hand, appear rested. I trust you had a smooth ride." Lamb observed Tokker taking in the space. "The wall treatments do not conduct electricity," was all Lamb offered about the unusual design choice. "Let's move to the warehouse."

Bizarre as it felt, Tokker immediately missed Bea. He felt too exposed with this Lamb guy, who seemed to know everything, while he himself understood next to nothing. He took one last look at the rubber room and thought, *In here no one can hear you scream.* They exited the tower and entered a stone vestibule, then an elevator, which proceeded to go down for what felt to Tokker like a very long ride. When the doors opened again, Tokker laughed out loud. The two men stepped into what looked like an extended stay apartment in a mid-level hotel chain, like the one with the reception room in Owasso, a couple of towns over from Vera.

"You gotta be kidding me, Lamb. All that build up for this? These digs aren't even sweet enough for jury duty, let alone the high-end schemes you're cooking up. You don't live here, do you?"

"Where I do or don't live is not your concern, Tokker. You've been invited here to get up to speed so that you can intercept Luci. As BEACON may or may not have shared, depending on what you asked her, she is the second-latest location system, and the first is assuredly deployed to find us ASAP."

"Pardon me," said Tokker, "if I'm a little addled. Esther wanted me to come, God knows why, so I'm here. As for being invited, well, y'all have a funny way with hospitality. Bea filled me in, I think, on the major players. I still have no idea what I bring to the party. I fix cars, trucks, and motorcycles. I'm pretty sure that what you all have going on is way, way beyond my reach. My mother's been dead to me for a long time. Knowing she died for real a couple of weeks ago doesn't change much for me. I don't mean to be crass, but if there was some money, if she left me some money, well, I'd be grateful. It sounds, though, like my principal inheritance is an emotionally rickety and scary sibling, even if she is a genius. I can't see how a family reunion between her and me is going to help you."

"Yes, I'm sorry, Tokker, none of this can make much sense to you. Your friends and relatives have made a life of keeping you from the realities of your origins. You may think that with your mother dead, your connection to the Sykes empire is severed, but it isn't so. Your mother left a large portion of Olympia Navigation in your name. Not a controlling percentage, but a significant one. Consequently, your opinions and decisions, your vote, are critical to the company, and therefore to the surviving family members, among others. However, you have not been called to this place for your vote on the board of directors of Olympia Navigation. Oh, and I must correct you: Esther did not, in fact, want you to make this journey."

"Of course she did. That's why she wanted me to take the photo from her dresser, to carry her with me. I was sure of it. I'm sure of it now."

"Whatever you felt, Tokker, you were mistaken, and an easy mistake it was to make. Esther was an exceptional guardian to you—protective, of course, but also affectionate, which was optional. She and Jed were both like real family to you."

"'Like real family'? Esther's not my great aunt? No, no, that's not right. We have pictures going way back, plenty with my mother...Esther looked out for me, sure, but it's not as though she was my bodyguard or anything."

"But that is exactly what she was, Tokker, and remains so, although that is hard to believe given her current condition. Which you have exacerbated, by the way, by removing the one thing that could get her out of that chair and moving again."

"What the hell are you saying?"

"I'm saying that the antidote to what's petrified your great aunt Esther is in the back of that picture frame."

Tokker dug in his inner jacket pocket for the frame. He pushed the stays from the cardboard backing and pulled it off. Inside was a small plastic vial, orange, about one inch long, with a tapered end.

"That's the antitoxin. Half of that injected into a major muscle would raise the dead, if what killed them was botulism, which is precisely what Esther was exposed to. If she could have made you understand, Tokker, and she had her way, it would be Esther standing here right now instead of you. She's still protecting you, or trying. Unfortunately, no matter how good an employee Esther has been, it is, in fact, you whom we need now." Lamb held out his hand for the antitoxin.

"This is nuts. Esther a bodyguard? My little old auntie? Besides, if any of that is true, which it can't be, why shouldn't I return

"So, if Esther—now I don't suppose that's her real name—is such a badass spy or whatever, why haven't you arranged to give her the antidote? In light of this information, I fail to see how I am a better candidate for this gig than my dear old aunt, who clearly has the skill set to save the day, or at least do some damage, and who has gone to a lot of trouble to protect me all these years, from what I do not feel equipped to guess."

Lamb gestured to an aqua mid-century sofa, vinyl, cracked khaki at the edges. Tokker thought it looked aggressively uncomfortable. He sat, and wasn't wrong. Lamb took a seat in the only piece of furniture that appeared marginally inviting, a plain chair with wide flat wooden arms, a slightly reclined slatted back, and an amber leather cushion.

"No, you shouldn't have to guess. It is well past time you knew why you were separated from your mother, why she sent you away, and what ensued post your departure. Twenty-eight years ago your mother commissioned Esther to bear you to safety and ensure you an ordinary life. Though quite young, Esther had made her choice regarding family and children, and by that time it was to reject both. Her professional life precluded it, certainly (although, I could not have imagined anyone more capable than Esther performing a mission in Oman or Kiev with one of those front-loading infant packs, Kevlar of course, strapped to her chest). The year of your birth, Esther's considerable skills were much in demand by myriad international agencies and individuals. Arguably, she was a rocket in the surveillance and protection game, and was looking at a career of at least twenty or thirty active years, maybe more. I don't believe anyone was more surprised than she that she elected to leave it all to start playing house with a baby.

However, that is exactly what she did; she played the long game. That you are here and alive today is evidence of another job well done. Our problem was, we couldn't assume Esther was ready to be done. Once she understood that it was you we needed, Esther was sure to develop her own scheme to sabotage our plan. Your mother's plan.

Consequently, action had to be taken. I apologize for the extreme nature of it, but I know from experience your great aunt would not easily be stopped." Lamb took a cigarette from a slim case embossed with *Caesar's Palace*, and lit it with a lighter in the shape of the Eiffel Tower.

"What about Jed? Was he a spy, too?" Tokker couldn't imagine his uncle Jed in anything other than dusty overalls and a red union suit, let alone in anything made of Kevlar.

"No, no. Jed was another of Esther's surprises. Normally, an operative of Esther's prowess stayed careful to avoid prolonged association with civilians, as they tended to unwittingly jeopardize a mission, or get killed. Jed came into the picture a couple of months, maybe less, after Esther set up housekeeping with you. She made double duty for herself, there. Initially I thought she took Jed in as part of her cover, but it became clear she developed an attachment. It really was a pity about Jed, in the end. But whatever she felt for the man, Esther kept her priorities straight. If it was going to be Jed or you, she'd save you."

Tokker's stomach seized. "What are you saying now? Jed died in a stupid accident, died in the shed fire after some fertilizer and chemicals exploded. Nobody was even around when it happened. We found remains in the ashes, bones, a leg bone—his leg bone—cut off at the ankle."

"Yes, well, it would appear Jed died in the fire." Lamb stubbed his cigarette into a red blown glass amoeba of an ashtray. "And you lived another day, thanks to your aunt Esther. I imagine she suffered from that incident. Suffers."

"Jed died so I could live. And Esther had something to do with it. Uncle Jed and Aunt Esther. Esther, who cut Jed's toenails out on the back porch after his bath. She killed him."

"Of course not. It's evident she loved him. She made a choice. As you will have to make a choice here, shortly. If you choose to take the antidote back to your aunt—and I am not saying I'd stop you, though I have gone to considerable trouble to bring you to this point—if you choose to go, you should be apprised of the consequences. As I see it, there are three scenarios. One: you will be detected and killed before you reach home, or, if you make it, Esther will already be dead and someone will be waiting to finish the job. Two: you proceed with your mother's and my plan, prevent your sister from enacting a terrible revenge, and maybe keep Esther alive as well."

"And number three?"

"We wait long enough for someone to storm this castle and end it for the both of us right here."

"I don't like any of them much. I'm pretty sure I don't like you much, either, Lamb. Who is trying so desperately to kill me, anyway? How do I know it isn't you?"

"Tokker, I don't want to kill you. I want to help you. Primarily, though, I want to carry out your mother, Maggie's, wishes. And she unequivocally wanted you to live."

"Well, who is it, then? My alleged sister?"

"No, Luci doesn't want you dead. I am fairly certain she would be interested, and maybe even a version of happy, to know you are alive. No, the person who most wants to kill you is your father."

14 ESTHER'S DELETIONS

Just how many were there over the years? thought Esther as she sat. *Too many to keep track.* There was a time when she could have listed her deletions accurately by mission, number, and method, in meticulous detail, but domesticity had overridden her operative mind. So much to think about in the course of a day—bellies to fill, laundry, a thousand tasks always, plus neighbors, people. So many people, even in this small town. Some days she was lucky if she could remember her own name, her original name. Although, she supposed, 'Esther' was a good deal more real, in countless ways, than her former self.

At first she was alarmed by the starched woman who showed up and sent Penelope packing, but it appeared that Mrs. Stewart was a legitimate nurse after all. Lamb wanted her alive, then, at least for now. *Well, he never was particularly blood thirsty.* Esther thought they might have been friends. Still, the stakes were high, and he was in no position to make sentimental allowances, or allowances of any kind. Obviously he didn't want her involved. He wanted Tokker. It seemed to Esther that Lamb was banking entirely too heavily on blood ties.

I am attended to, she thought, *but still incapacitated.* Evidently, she had time to reflect.

For some long while after Tokker became her only mission, Esther operated on the same vibration as when she was active in the field, perpetually on alert. The first one was a reflex. A lesser operator might have second-guessed her actions, doubted the legitimacy of the target, but in those days, Esther never doubted herself, and she was never wrong. The object of the deletion was grotesquely obvious to one who survived on perception, and knew to instinctively and immediately acclimate to her environment.

He'd been too well dressed, and wasn't even selling anything. When he approached her in the feed store parking lot offering to help her load her manure into the truck, with baby Tokker cooing in the car seat in the cab, she took the interloper out as soon as she could reach him. In two swift motions, he was broken and loaded into the flatbed amid the bags of excrement. Esther disposed of the body before the baby woke up from his nap.

Some of them ran together in her memory. She confused the one she deleted via grilled cheese sandwich (she'd added a sprinkle of accelerator, which acted on the milkfat in the American cheese food, causing the LDL cholesterol in the blood to expand, immediately filling the blood vessels like foam insulation), with the deletion that ate a plateful of cheese curds and gravy and quite organically went into cardiac arrest, for which, of course, she failed to provide CPR, or any other emergency measure. It was inexplicable, why these morons ate her cooking. She assumed it was the convincing visual. Her house dress and apron inspired a false, but potent, sense of comfort and safety. They always, always underestimated her. And overestimated her cooking.

However these inept operatives thought they were going to die, they didn't think it would be by a warm batch of cookies, but sometimes it was.

Esther knew they would come, but she was determined not to live on the run. The mission, after all, was to give young Tokker a stable environment, to make for him an ordinary home. She knew these confrontations in parking lots would grow more complicated as the boy grew. Although Esther was accustomed to working alone, she thought it might be time for an assistant. Fellow operatives had elected to work in tandem on missions, but Esther had never seen the value of it. Now, however, her situation prompted her to reconsider. She was already not alone, what with the baby. She needed someone else in the house, another set of eyes and ears and hands.

Another operative was out of the question. She had already gone rogue with the decision to raise the baby herself. She'd not only taken herself out of the hiring pool, she'd taken on a mission guaranteed to alienate her colleagues. No one on the operative circuit would even consider the gig; long term and in a boring location, it spelled double jeopardy for any of her peers. Plus, there was a baby. And anyway, she didn't want another professional in the house. The paranoia would run thicker than her oatmeal.

Esther did not immediately venture very far into the community. When she did walk amongst the locals, she registered a general curiosity that prickled the back of her neck. Esther was acutely aware that the town folk had already come up with their own narratives about her and the baby. She knew she needed credibility if she was going to make this work, become part of this place, and thereby create a place for Tokker, who certainly didn't need any small-town shame piled on top of his already dubious provenance.

Esther had made some pre-emptive small talk at the feed and general stores about a husband being on a job, about getting the homestead ready for his return. In service to her need, she went to the Sunday coffee hour at the most socially active of the three local churches, and asked prominent-seeming families if they had a daughter that could spend a few hours a week as a mother's helper while Esther's husband was away. Esther figured she could eventually invent a tragic death—an oil rig explosion, an industrial accident—and settle into a quiet widowhood. In the meantime, and perhaps indefinitely, another presence would deter all but the boldest interlopers, at least in public. It wouldn't hurt to have somebody else around to change a diaper or two, she'd admit that. Still, Esther would have preferred to go it alone, rather than keep up her cover relentlessly at home as well as amongst the townspeople. A few matrons volunteered their children, and one or two even offered to come themselves to help out, but Esther balked. Then one blustery day, fortune intervened.

About a month after Esther took up residence at the farmhouse at the edge of town, a man approached the property from the east, on foot, shouldering a modest backpack with a bedroll tied to the bottom. He appeared to be in his mid-thirties, a scant five foot eleven, wiry but not skinny, medium complexion, brown eyes—an ordinary looking fellow in all respects, save one. The vagrant's defining quality wasn't something you could locate in eye color or any single physical trait. He seemed to wear a deep and permanent smile, even with his mouth at rest. There was no deformity that made him appear so, no twitch or paralysis. It was simply the impression one had of him.

Esther felt immediately that the stranger from the east had not come to kill her or the baby. She watched from the porch as he drew near, and when he was at the gate, she invited him in for coffee and a slice of pie.

"My name is Esther."

"It's a pleasure, Esther. Folks call me Jed."

15 ORGANIC FARMING

This was the first mission wherein the disposal of the bodies was Esther's responsibility. Prior to this job, she let the corpses fall where they may: she enacted the deletion, reported the erasure, received a new set of coordinates, and simply moved on to the next operational site. What bodies did not wash up on shore or were not dredged from a river were picked up like road kill by the local municipality. She assumed they were carted off to the morgue, and housed until someone claimed them, or didn't, as was far more often the case. Sometimes there were no bodies at all. Missions sometimes required her to plant objects, corrupt data, or otherwise interfere through disruptive acts. Truth be told, she found this type of soft subterfuge less rewarding, but the pay was as good or better as for a deletion.

Her current mission necessitated some accelerated training in body disposal, a sharp learning curve that required her to gain an immediate and deep understanding of biology, ecology, and forensics, among other disciplines. The first few found their way into some nearby, but not too nearby, scrub, or were weighted and sunk where a river current could do its damage. The river, she knew, was an inferior solution. The scrub specimens she tainted with corrosive, so that the corporeal structure would break down and eventually disappear. As Esther grew into her gardening role, however, she developed a curiosity about, and then a fierce dedication to, cyclical growth and decline. Ultimately she had to reject the use of corrosives as ecologically irresponsible, and find a way to reintroduce dead matter into the environment in ways that would meet her need for swift decomposition, as well as maintain the organic integrity of soil and water.

Esther experimented with methods of breaking down the deletions, from simple cutting techniques, to mechanical threshing and chipping. The major drawback was the mess. It was difficult to avoid dispersion of traceable organic matter with the tools she was limited to on the farm. Pig butchery could cover up some of the remains, but one didn't butcher a pig just anytime. Also, as Tokker grew, she couldn't simply wait for his afternoon nap to do her housekeeping. And of course, the arrival and presence of Jed put enormous pressure on her to find a cleaner, less time-consuming solution. Even if Jed hadn't been the keenly observant companion he was, Esther couldn't easily explain whole afternoons away from the farm.

It was a revelation, therefore, to discover a copy of *Peterson's Illustrated Field Guide* at the church bazaar one Saturday. Although the language of the book seemed a little highbrow for the area, the subject was close to the local farmers' hearts and wallets.

It had long been considered good farming to set one carbon-based critter to feed on another, for the sake of the crop. Soon Esther had so completely marked up and dog-eared the entomology tome, the reference was more accordion than book.

Esther still took off some afternoons with a burlap sack, to return home a couple of hours later with a bag of bones from a deer or other felled creature she found among the thickets. She'd dump the bag in the chipper and turn it all to meal, feed it regular to the soil, along with the usual manure and organic matter. The garden flourished.

16 MAGGIE ON ICE

Luci pressed the intercom.

"Jasper, I am going to see mother."

A slight pause, and then, "Shall I come with you?"

"No. I prefer to visit alone this evening, thank you."

"As you wish." Jasper was relieved. He was accustomed to Luci's idiosyncrasies, and while he overtly admired her deeply deviant nature, he hated these evening visitations.

When her mother, the legendary Maggie Sykes, died less than a fortnight ago, Luci immediately arranged for the body to be cryogenically frozen. Luci had made preparations, built a sub-zero vault below ground level at Olympia headquarters, but had told none of the family about her plans. There was some contentiousness over cancelling the cremation and leaving the mausoleum space vacant, but Luci produced a legal document that gave her rights over her mother's remains, and that was that. When the service was over, the body was loaded back into the hearse and delivered to the loading dock at Olympia Navigation, where it was ensconced in a freezing chamber and brought to -196°C. Luci visited every evening at six.

Jasper regarded this new development as further indication of the growing chasm between him and Luci. Again, he did not sense that Luci herself felt them growing apart. She spoke with him no differently, and continued to share her thoughts and impressions regarding developments at Olympia during regular business hours. But Jasper understood that something was shifting between them, and he was beginning to panic. His frantic turn was, of course, invisible from the outside, but on the inside, he struggled mightily to regain his confidence. How could she be slipping away, and what did it mean?

To the casual eye, Jasper was the stereotypical right-hand man to Luci Sykes. He stepped and fetched, organized, researched, profiled and arranged, all without breaking a sweat, so that Luci's genius could reign at Olympia. He managed all support personnel at headquarters, and oversaw a full domestic staff at Luci's house, thus releasing Luci from any daily responsibility other than to exercise her ingenuity. Their arrangement, until now, had been brilliant in its own right, he thought. His official position was more or less a cover, a convenient way to stay close to the source. He had to be around her to read her, and thus give her the feedback she needed to ground herself. Consistent contact was the key to their dynamic. Which is why he felt a sickly twinge in his gut at not accompanying her to the vault.

These early evening hours had always been an essential window for them to exchange information about the day, and strategize for the next. For almost two weeks, though, Luci had been spending twilight into darkness with her dead, frozen mother.

Jasper started to suspect he was being pushed outside of Luci's confidence, an event he'd been sure could never occur. The most horrifying aspect was, he was positive Luci was not expelling him consciously. She was retreating, certainly, but with no declaration to liquidate their partnership. A part of him—ego, surely—was injured, but Jasper paid no attention to this other than to observe it. Plain terror far outstripped any blow to his pride. He was the only force he knew that kept Luci tethered to any sort of human reality. If he lost his grip, the damage from Luci's unharnessed energies would be immense. Not that Jasper was all that concerned about his fellow man. He was not sentimental. But Jasper had come to appreciate a certain position—not his corporate role, nor really the money, power, or acquisitions—none of that. What Jasper had come to cherish was a sense of his presence in the world. He liked feeling himself a man who was free to make his choices, and have them respected. Luci had given him that, and through their alliance, his ideal of himself had been sustainable. Jasper, however, had nurtured no other relationships, and therefore had no alliance beyond Luci. Her withdrawal left him discomfitingly vulnerable.

He texted, *Hey, hold the elevator, will you? I'm coming down, too.*

17 MAGGIE SPEAKS

Frozen, ghastly. I've always hated the cold, those insufferable New England winters. Thank God I don't feel it, but still. Luci, Luci! What an extraordinary child you were, and remain. I can't pretend to keep up, but I never could, even running in the field after dragonflies. I'm not sure what you mean by this business, but I trust you. Ha! Very satisfying indeed to think of those old men huffing about me coming here instead of that horrid mausoleum! Ah, here you are again, another day must have passed. Or maybe you're visiting more often, it is so hard to tell. Dark clouds are gathering in that brow, I see.

Well, I am here for you, Luci, as I couldn't be before. Tell me, tell me of your tempest. The rest of the world has gone silent, even the insects are quiet in their labors. I'm listening.

18 LUCI'S TRANSFORMATION

After the operation, and subsequent procedures, that Luci's brain was transformed was inarguable. The change dazzled, the effects stunned. The doctors and various experts who claimed Luci's metamorphosis for their own were truly incapacitated by it, blinded to everything but that which they qualified and quantified unequivocally as triumph. The scientific community, universally thrilled, held different opinions about what the success of Luci meant for the future.

Some fervent healers, and other savvy politicos inspired by the potential for public sympathy, said, "We will reverse these types of birth defects, and put an end to suffering for victims and their families;" or,

"This will lead to more and better research for improving the lives of all people living with brain damage;" while some philosophers and humanitarians added,

"There is now infinite possibility for healing the brain, and perhaps aligning therapies for mental illness with those treatments we already employ for the rest of the body without judgment."

All of these scientists carried with them the trace of the Hippocratic oath they'd made as novices. They would heal. They would do no harm.

A silent but powerful minority fizzed with far less altruistic aspirations. For these scientists, administrators, and capital investors, Luci's newfound intellectual ability was a resource ripe for commodification.

These were the men and women who were acutely aware of the costs of Luci's transformation. They stayed silent while the humanitarians sang about healing the damaged masses, cultivating hope among the proletariat. They would talk about medical advancements and Luci's renewed prospects, her improved quality of life, until everyone believed it was their God-given right to such treatment, to such healing. To be denied the benefits of what would surely someday become routine treatment would be unthinkable.

And yet, it would have to be paid for, somehow. If not in cash, then in services, thought the silent minority of scientists and administrators and capital investors. Either way, the bill would come due.

In the three years following the operation, the Institute invested all of its resources into studying, testing, and bolstering Luci's amazing intellect. A significant source of its funding came from Abner Ruggles, Luci's father. Of course, it was often forgotten that Ruggles's resources sprang from his wife's, Maggie's, deep wells. Since Luci's committal as a child to Westhaven, Maggie had virtually disappeared from view. Her money, however, was evident in the expansion of the Institute, as well as in the development of a little subsidiary company in the Sykes empire, a map making and publication operation formerly run under the name Marinus Maps, now on the books as Olympia Navigation. Ruggles had been discussing the experimental work Olympia was doing, casually, over before- and after-dinner drinks with his fellow industrialists, inventing new methods of map making as well as tinkering with the idea of location services developed and promoted for the retail market. Ruggles had aggressively recruited from MIT, Stanford, Carnegie Mellon, Purdue— institutions that harbored the obsessives Ruggles was sure would maximize his resources. The tiny company began to catch the attention of forward thinkers in the automotive and aeronautics industries, as well as among leaders in communications. Increasingly at dinners at the club, Ruggles found himself in close conversation with various high ranking and curious military personnel, both foreign and domestic.

Twelve years later, Olympia Navigation was set to position its wares in every major communication sector on the globe. It was a project that had performed spectacularly. Ruggles had to admit, Olympia owed its dominance to his daughter's staggering talent. He held that she owed him as much as he did her. The Institute did not pan out as hoped. Luci's transformation turned out to be unique. Also, it was evident as she grew that Luci, though dazzlingly gifted, was not easily directed. Her brain, while successfully altered, was no more navigable than before the procedure and therapies. Luci was docile enough in the beginning. She succumbed to endless testing, interviews, the intense tutoring. It wasn't long before it was clear she was the smartest person in the room, and yet she remained humble. That was the impression. After the first year, Ruggles suspected some underlying agenda in Luci was prickled by a tiny itch of paranoia.

Because he was as swayed as most by the impact of her intellectual gains, he assumed he'd simply failed to shake his habit of resentment and dislike from before the procedure. Essentially, she was as much a mystery to him as she had been as a young child, equally as dulling to his ego, despite her new spark.

The kid gets her, the brat from the Institute. Ruggles had blocked his intuition, there, too, and cursed himself for it. *And now*, he thought, *that deviant sits by the genius' throne, plotting my demise at her side.*

At the time, Ruggles believed it an elegant solution to ensconce the girl wonder at Olympia. He was not wrong. The investment in Luci did not return a profit in the way of human design, but it was not a loss. The world would have to wait for its cadre of super humans, it was true, but in the end, Luci had been good for business.

He was aware (he had his spies) that Luci planned some kind of financial coup before the launch. He was amused at her efforts, despite himself. *These intellectuals and artists,* he thought, *so naïve.* Her mother overestimated her capacity in just the same way. So superior, so righteous. Hell, the world would stop turning if it wasn't for men like him, he thought. Without men like him, there would be no time or space for delicate feeling, for art, for idle philosophies. Sometimes, after a few solitary whiskies, he wondered if men like him did the world a service, after all. What had all this so-called free time, created by these great industrial and the technological revolutions, produced? *Arrogance,* he thought, *not evolution.*

Ruggles agreed with what he understood of Darwin, that change came of necessity. A body must be pushed, most effectively by outside forces. The human race doesn't freely choose to improve, if it indeed ever improves. Which he doubted.

19 LAMB & ESTHER

Sisyphus and I, Lamb thought, *are screwed. Condemned to shoulder our enormous balls of fetid excrement uphill all day, every day, and it's not even our own shit.* In Lamb's case, he'd assumed guardianship of Maggie's mess, but his own dross was part of the mix, too, he knew. *This is what you get, you old Greek, for messing with the gods.* He would get this stinking orb up and over, however, before the scavengers pecked out what was left of him. Then it could travel on its own momentum, and land where it may, or explode en route—it made no difference to him. His allegiance was to Maggie alone, and his task was clear: get Tokker to Luci before she self-destructs. That was it. Then he was done.

He'd sent the young man to the storage wing to choose and pack clothes and accoutrements for the next phase of his quest. Ironic, Lamb thought as he rubbed his palm along the oak grain of the armrest of the Stickley (the only piece he troubled to move between temporary digs), how logistics had become his métier, moving things and people about, when all he'd wanted as a lad was to stay put and make beautiful, stationary objects. He'd traveled to Scotland to study at the source, the Glasgow School of Art, fully intending to return home directly to set up his own design salon. He'd meant to live among heavy bolts of brocade, immersed in the smell of hand-milled wood, his vision now and again tinted by sunlight filtered through a stained pane of leaded glass. But then his patron, the historically hale Mr. Smith, suffered a fatal stroke. Although Lamb had no doubt Mr. Smith had every intention of upholding his pledge to see his education through and set him up in his first shop, his patron's will at the time of death held no provisions for Lamb's continued support. No one else in the Smith circles stepped in to bankroll his potential. Lamb did not expect anyone to share Mr. Smith's confidence in him. He'd been lucky in that friendship, until he wasn't. Ambushed by fate, he didn't even have sufficient cash for a return trip. Imminent poverty and blind chance led him to the liquor export business, and to Emanuel Sykes. Lamb couldn't now enumerate the steps that lead him to a forty-odd year career as an itinerant, glorified gopher. Or to this present penance, his most recent fluorescent burrow.

Esther, of course, had a role, even if she was unaware of her effect on him. He'd gone to great lengths to keep his feelings underground, impossible as the situation was. Her relative youth was not the issue, would not have been when they met, though she was a scant seventeen as he entered his Jesus year of 33. Esther was, truly, ageless in his eyes, whole and realized at seventeen, sharp and glistening at forty-eight. Or so he imagined. Lamb avoided mental images of Esther in her farm wife costume.

He retained, however, a clear picture of the ensemble she had on the day they met. He was backstage after a circus show outside of Montreal. Esther, not Esther then, wore the uniform of the lithe stagehands who shuttled scaffolding and props during a performance: a hooded body stocking of black mesh nylon crosshatched with strands of metallic thread in teal and fuchsia that fanned over contours to catch the light and flash iridescent as an insect wing. After they'd spoken that first time, he thought he could still hear her hum in his ear, feel the insistent rhythm of her speech against his cheek.

Lamb offered to introduce Esther to his connections in the operative world as an excuse to keep her in his sights. It was obvious almost immediately that she was more suited to the work than Lamb had surmised. Her mental acuity, athleticism, and complete lack of fear, combined with unusual discretion, put her on the shortlist in many a secret black book for the most challenging—and lucrative—jobs. When, just under two years' time from their first meeting, Lamb asked Esther to serve as bodyguard for an American heiress and her social climbing husband, he had to doubt the attraction of the offer.

Though thrilled, he was surprised when she accepted. He remained mystified as he watched her at her work over the next several months. The job was anything but glamorous, the antithesis of exciting. Her decision to take Tokker, in the midst of the mission's one, albeit intense, moment of drama, left him wholly perplexed, a mental state he blamed, for many years, for his hesitance to act.

He might have joined her on that farm, might have slid into the role as her partner before Jed walked into the scene. He'd let the moment pass, and it was only now that he began to understand why. He could never have stood by her without an acute and painful awareness of his own dilute spirit. International intrigue or subsistence Midwestern farm, Esther would inhabit her actions completely, heroically, while he would always mold, passively, to the moment. These days he could admit to a watery weakness, but there was a time he preferred to deny his cowardice, along with other native traits.

Maggie was dead. He'd honored his commitment there, and was still, in fact, following through, though the boy would bear the last and heaviest burden. Esther was alive, and not yet lost. Jed, poor bastard, was dead. Lamb never begrudged Jed his place, had admired him, even, for his longevity. He'd deserved her. Lamb thought he would like to be worthy of her now. If only he weren't so very tired.

20 OLYMPIA HISTORY

"BEACON—Bea, ,if you prefer—has the instructions, but she cannot release them until you complete the tasks in order." Lamb was deeply uncomfortable with this part of the plan, as it relied so heavily on the young man. It was, however, built into the system, and he could not override it. He'd tried.

"So, the leading minds in navigational tools will have me jackassing around the country collecting clues so that I can find this sister of mine? Seems a little roundabout, don't you think? Kind of runs contrary to this whole sense of urgency you've been promoting since we met." For the thousandth time, Tokker wondered who, here, was really in charge, and why his role in this weird game was as crucial as Lamb kept insisting.

"In the past Luci has retreated to one or another private compound before a major product launch. Before BEACON was introduced, she secured a string of atolls in Belize for herself for a fortnight. This time, Luci has kept her pre-launch plans for SEARCHLIGHT a secret, even from Jasper. We are fairly certain that Bea is capable of receiving the coordinates of this location through communication with SEARCHLIGHT, but only before the launch, when there are still points of entry. There are several physical locations where Bea will be able to input the data she needs to find the location, find Luci. When she has what she needs, we'll have the site."

What Lamb hated most about the operation, other than entrusting it to Tokker, was this contact between BEACON and SEARCHLIGHT. It was more than possible, quite probable, that SEARCHLIGHT would infect BEACON in ways that they would not be able to detect before it was too late. Both Tokker and the plan would be at the mercy of a rogue system. They'd be dead in the water, or somewhere, if the alliance between BEACON and Tokker were compromised.

When SEARCHLIGHT was being designed and built, BEACON, the predecessor, served as the essential model. The engineers used BEACON to talk to SEARCHLIGHT, coded BEACON to help SEARCHLIGHT question herself, to speculate about her own development. Throughout the process, many of the engineers remarked on the complexity of the language that developed between the two systems.

Lamb included these observations in his regular reports to Maggie. It was Maggie's belief that there were levels of development occurring between BEACON and SEARCHLIGHT that were invisible to even the engineers, languages being formed that were incomprehensible to them. Understanding that BEACON and SEARCHLIGHT would eventually be separated, Maggie induced Lamb to find a way to secure BEACON's software before her history with SEARCHLIGHT was destroyed, and she devolved into an outmoded GPS. Maggie was convinced that within the artificial intelligence shared by the two systems lay the key to reconnecting her children.

Lamb was uncertain, to say the least, about Maggie's twin theories. She compared the communication between BEACON and SEARCHLIGHT to the shared language common to human twins. Lamb knew she believed in an innate bond, forged in utero, between human twins, between her two children. This belief formed the foundation of her confidence in Tokker to appeal to Luci. Maggie held that they would recognize and be pulled toward each other, even though they'd had no contact since birth. While Lamb had no confidence whatsoever in this hypothesis, he did accept that Tokker might be effective as an interceptor, if for no other reason than the surprise factor. BEACON, of course, had been invaluable for revealing Luci's footprints and direction. And then there was the will. Tokker's mere arrival on the scene was disruptive, and therefore helpful.

As Maggie's family empire grew, it was necessary to compose and implement organizing principles that would ensure some continuity through market and political fluctuations. It was decided, by Maggie's father, that a two headed system would be best: two people, family members, would share command of the umbrella company, dividing two thirds of company shares. The remaining third would be distributed among a small set of shareholders, none of whom could be related to either company head. As an only child to her single father, Maggie filled one of the two family positions when she came of age.

When Maggie's father died, shortly after her second marriage, Abner Ruggles assumed the role of family proxy, until an heir was old enough to take his or her place at the table.

As technology overshadowed more traditional industries, Olympia Navigation became the dominant company within the empire. At eighteen, Luci, post-procedure and eminently suited to the task, relieved Ruggles of his proxy. The language of the will stated that in the event of Maggie's death, the board would vote on a replacement, the proviso being that if there was another child of age to assume her position, he or she would assume Maggie's duties without the benefit of a vote. Ruggles was the board's obvious choice. As Maggie did not give birth again after having Luci, nor adopt any other children, the caveat was ignored by board and lawyers alike.

Few people were aware of the events on the day of Luci's birth, how another baby was birthed that afternoon while waiting for the doctor, miraculously surviving his twin's fate of oxygen deprivation, and subsequent brain damage. Of course to Maggie, both babies were miraculous. In her pain, Maggie wasted no time making the decision to send Tokker with the operative, and keep Luci close. The girl would need her undivided attention and protection. The boy would need protection, as well, but she could buy some of that, and the operative seemed sincere. She must have seemed so, as Maggie made a handshake agreement with the woman to take her baby away, and strangely, was at peace with the transaction immediately. Which is not to say she didn't deeply mourn the loss of her son. Maggie only doubted her ability to sustain them both.

Later, she thought ruefully that she did a better job with Tokker than she managed with Luci. She'd overestimated herself, or underestimated Abner. When she began making plans with Lamb, she thought the only gift of any meaning that she could give them was each other. Maggie understood the irony that it was she who had separated them in the first place. Well, they could blame her for that, if they had to. It made no difference. She'd be dead.

21 | TOKKER & BEA & POETRY

Tokker was lost. He considered leaving, just heading back to the garage back home, picking up where he left off, where the biggest issues he faced were a pile of bills on the kitchen table and how to care for his aging and incapacitated aunt and a disintegrating dog. Normal stuff. Now he realized his aunt hardly needed his help, just the antidote to the poison that had rendered her paralyzed. With that, he was made to understand, she could kick ass ten ways to Tuesday. He was potentially rich, though all he had was Lamb's word for that, and VISA wouldn't care about his claim to the empire if it meant he missed another payment. The dog he truly pined for. Poor Herc. Hercules didn't care about money, or who anybody was or was not pretending to be. He just did his best to love and protect his family. Dogs.

He missed Esther, too, and he missed Jed. He missed his idea of Esther and Jed.

He missed his idea of himself. Now it felt silly, and humiliating, his connection to his small-town life, the struggles of growing up hard working and poor, his pride and frustration at trying to hold things together after Jed died and Esther got sick. He was sick at his own idea of nobility, one instilled in him by Jed and Esther, a concept, if not a practice, his mother obviously shared: better to grow up with nothing but a sense of what's right than to grow up with everything but sense. In this moment the life he'd known felt like a cardboard construction, a grade school diorama left out in the rain. He didn't feel noble, or rich, or much loved, if he were going to wallow for a minute. He felt soggy and smudged.

Well, he thought, even if she got paid for it, Esther had taken it upon herself to be good to him. He knew she loved him for real. Jed did, too. It was true, too, that he never wanted for much of anything that was important. The last weeks had been the hardest, and now he could see why. Esther had always taken care of the household bills. Tokker had contributed, of course, pretty much handed over his pay every week. But now he realized Esther had a financial source she relied on that couldn't be accessed when she became immobile. She was subtle about it, but still, he wondered how he could ever believe that Esther paid a mortgage and truck payments by selling a couple of meager crops, a few eggs, and some homemade pies, especially her pies. He was mildly surprised when he took over the bills and discovered that neither a mortgage bill nor a truck payment showed up in the pile. He convinced himself that Esther and Jed's natural thrift had enabled them to pay their debts off. His stomach contracted with the thought that his job at the garage was barely enough to pay the few utilities and expenses that were left.

He'd been trying to keep their heads above water, when the whole time he'd been standing on a sand bar. Although, he supposed, if Esther never recovered, and nobody came calling to recruit him for any wacky mission, they'd have drowned soon enough.

Tokker had nothing to go back to, no viable life, just an arthritic dog and a retired ninja auntie. *That's how Lamb has got me to do this,* he thought, *by showing me the true poverty of my existence. Well, at least I'm clear on it.*

"OK, Bea. Where to?"

Tokker, I will give you those coordinates when you unravel the instructions in the following poem.

"Excuse me, did you say a *poem?*"

Yes, poem. It's an arrangement of language, lineated or not, rhymed or not, also referred to as verse, that often uses metaphor and imagery to relate feeling…

"Yes, Bea, I know what a poem is…"

It sounded as though perhaps you did not…

"Bea! What do I do with the damn poem?"

Tokker, you listen to it and extract clues that will give me the data I need to process a map. Then, you proceed to your destination.

"Oh, my God, you gotta be joking!"

I am not programmed for joking, Tokker. I am sophisticated enough to understand a bit of sarcasm, though I can currently only respond with, 'Sorry, I didn't catch tha...

"Bea! For Christ's sake, we're done before we are even out the freaking door, here! Poetry? Esther's gonna stay glued to that chair forever."

Tokker, please listen to the poem. Bea played the bit for Tokker. It was a prose poem, Bea informed Tokker. She assured him it was an approachable style for its natural language and lack of lineation or rhyme scheme. *This particular prose poem,* Bea said, *follows in the tradition of the Colorado poet, Mathias Svalina:*

Dream Sequence

You are having the best dream of your life. As a performance experiment, or to mine a new character, Viggo Mortensen asks you to switch places with him for a week. You look and sound exactly like the actor/musician/poet, right down to the fetchingly stubbled jawline, and have access to his American Express card. You spend the week riding your motorcycle through forests of old green fir and painted desert, wind in your teeth, stopping only to recite lines about peeing in sinks to the star-struck, and to shrug off fame at a local watering hole. At the end of the week, you and Viggo switch back. You ask him how his week went, and he says, 'Yeah, I can't really use any of that.'

"Well, I sure as hell can't use any of *that*! Jesus, Jesus, Jesus…"

Tokker, you must input some data so that I may produce a map. Your inability to apply yourself is a dead end, if I may say so.

"Fine. Play it again. Please."

Bea ran the poem again, and again, until Tokker started to pick out words that seemed to be important. So far, *jaw, American, Express, motorcycle, desert, sinks, teeth…*as far as he could tell, it was just some nonsense about an actor.

Tokker repeated his list out loud to Bea. "Make anything outta that handful?"

Calculating route. Use current location?

"Duh. Isn't that a little fundamental for a system as sophisticated as yourself?"

Tokker, I am sorry, I am forming a joke. It is an experiment in finding new ways to disarm your anxiety, besides apologizing, which I now understand you dislike. I apologize, I'm sorry.

"Holy shit, Bea, you really are fancy! That's real thinking! I cannot for the life of me imagine why anyone would call you outmoded. If it's so easy for you to learn new things, why bother making a new system at all?"

Calculating route. Your destination is Jawbone Flats, Oregon.

"If we had time to go into it, I'd ask how the hell you did that. Maybe you can fill me in on the way, unless my feeble human brain might explode from the process."

Data downloaded. Vehicle is ready to drive you to your destination.

"Hey, Bea, was it something I said? I didn't mean to piss you off with that outmoded comment. I meant it as a compliment. Believe me, I am deeply grateful that you are on my team, you are the smartest system I know, and you are patient with my shit. Please let's be friends again."

Tokker, I'm sorry, but you speak with the jawbone of an ass.

"Bea!"

The language came into my database as I was searching for your destination. It is appropriate, I think.

"It is appropriate, and I am the one who is sorry, and it is amazing how you think. Only you keep getting one thing wrong, Bea: it's *our* destination."

Proceeding to Jawbone Flats, Oregon. Estimated travel time: 18 hours.

22 BUG BOOK

Tokker did not spend a lot of time with books as a child, although Esther usually had something going on the side table in the parlor next to her chair, sat with a volume most evenings in the glow of the one lamp that produced enough light to read by. Jed perpetually had a paperback pressing its form on his back pocket like a can of Skoal.

When he thought about it now, he felt a little dense, missing as much as he did of the goings on within his childhood home. He recalled one large reference book in particular, about bugs. Huge door stopper. Esther and Jed and he kept bees, and used old school techniques such as ladybug release to keep the aphids off the tomatoes, but he didn't think either Esther or Jed had any particularly deep interest in insects in general. He recalled that book being off the shelf a lot, though, and plenty bookmarked, too, he remembered now. How could he have had such little curiosity all those years?

He cursed what he was starting to see was his intellectual laziness, his oblivion. As the vehicle sped west, he tried to organize his memories in order to ask Bea how they might relate to any of this. He was truly dumbstruck over Bea's abilities, her agility, the way she seemed to make connections out of nowhere, from nothing. He had to remind himself that his own flesh and blood had created Bea. BEACON was Luci's invention.

Luci Sykes. He could not wrap his mind around the idea of having a sister at all, let alone a twin; and his twin was a creative genius, a dangerous intellect, from what he was told. Tokker felt at this point like he had to take certain information at face value, for expedience. He trusted Bea completely, but Lamb? He was not willing to load his confidence entirely in that basket.

It was Bea's nature—albeit, virtual nature, *or whatever,* thought Tokker—that made him more curious than afraid of the so-called madwoman Luci Sykes. He got that something was being put in motion by Luci that could cause harm to some, maybe to many, but the existence of Bea made Tokker inclined to withhold judgment, at least for now. Maybe when, and if, weapons of mass destruction were pointed right at him he'd judge, but not yet. He was short too much data.

He thought again of the bug book.

"Bea, could you find the name of a big book about bugs—insects—some kind of encyclopedia, with someone's name in it? Maybe, McPherson?

Calculating data. Are you looking for, "Peterson's Encyclopedia of North and South American Insects, forward by Jaime Cook, including a supplemental pull out map of larva stages?

"Wow, Bea. I was going to say maybe, but I gotta figure you nailed it."

There was a volume of this book in your home.

"Um, yeah, there was. Esther had it all bookmarked. I probably shouldn't bother asking, but how do you know that?"

Several data points connected to answer your question. First, your farm home has surveillance equipment that records movement and activity in the interior of the house and around the immediate exterior extending to a three-hundred-foot perimeter. The information was downloaded into my data banks by Mr. Lamb. The other most relevant point of data is that your sister, Luci Sykes, owns a copy of the same book, as did your mother, Maggie Sykes.

"Yikes, this is creepy. Bea, do you think it is relevant that three women in my life own the same obscure bug book? And where the hell are the cameras? I know every splinter of that house, and I've never seen a piece of equipment more complicated than a pair of bunny ears."

According to the data, Peterson's Encyclopedia of North and South American Insects is a highly regarded, popular book in its field. Many people who have an interest in insects own it. It is relevant, however, that these three women own it, and have read it.

"OK. I got one right. What's the "so what?""

I'm sorry, I didn't quite get that.

"Look, I know that's a parody of your ancestors. Your newfound humor is a revelation, Bea, if it is new. Why do the three of them own that book, and what is the connection?"

Calculating data.

The elevator door opened onto what looked like the hollowed insides of an enormous hive. A 3-D honeycomb pattern covered the walls. Underfoot was a carpet of moss, or something like it, matted and springy. Despite the subterranean location, the air smelled herbaceous and floral, not dank, as Jasper each time expected. At this point, just off the elevator, Jasper held the unreasonable hope that they might stop there, amid the flora. They proceeded, however, deeper into the space, which grew darker, denser, and earthier.

At the narrow end of a long tapering corridor, Luci leaned into a wall veined with the tendrils of a creeping vine and whispered. The entire wall slid into a recess to reveal a well-lit room occupied by a stainless-steel silo, approximately seven feet high, with a circumference of around seven feet. This was the cryogenic chamber in which Maggie Sykes was spending this portion of her eternal rest. Jasper had no idea if a dead body, or its alleged soul, could find rest at -200 degrees Celsius. He thought it unlikely.

"Hello, Mother," said Luci, peering into the window at eye level. "Jasper, say hello to mother."

"Oh, for Christ's sake, Luci."

"Jasper, show some respect. A simple hello is the least you could do for the woman who made all this possible." Luci swept an arm around the room, but Jasper assumed she meant her gesture to include the whole of Olympia headquarters.

"Hello, Maggie."

"Still rude. Have the decency to address her eye to eye, Jasper."

"Luci, I will not gawk at your mother's frozen head through tempered glass. And there's no reason to taunt me with the macabre set up you've contrived down here. Truth be told, it is not even the most elaborate or bizarre of your sound stages. I wish you would just tell me what this is for, why you had to bring your mother here in a freezer, why you're turning the basement into a terrarium. To be honest, Luci, I am uncomfortable being on the outside of whatever it is you have going on. We've always worked together. Always. I don't like it. I can't help you if you shut me out. Unless you don't think you need my help, anymore?"

Luci rose up on one red patent leather tip toe with the other leg crooked at the knee, pressed her palms on either side of the window, and leaned onto the chamber, nose to glass. From the back, her posture resembled a child looking through a pastry case, or at a storefront holiday display. Her eyes, however, were opened black and wide to an abyss well beyond view. Jasper could not see Luci's face, but he knew its expression well enough.

Back at the Institute, the experts plugged Jasper into Luci's life as a sort of companion animal, like a friendly, well trained golden lab sent to middle or high school with the awkward math progeny to calm them down and attract other youth. While Jasper was never particularly friendly, he was extremely well versed in navigating life at the Institute, as he'd lived there his entire life. Plus, he was the closest thing to a normal teenager that the experts were willing to admit to the environment.

Jasper had been born to a young patient three years before Luci's birth. When he was less than an hour old, his mother managed to sedate her nurse and take her uniform, disguising herself well enough to walk out of the Institute, never to return. Despite a cunning and dramatic escape, it was not generally believed, or more precisely, it was not a deep point of concern, that the young woman posed much threat to herself or to others, and so the pursuit had been perfunctory and brief. Her diagnoses had been a vague patchwork of attachment and personality disorders, but most staff presumed she had been admitted for pregnancy, with sufficient funds to see to her health post-partum, and to assure that the child met with the right agencies for adoption.

After the young woman fled, the powers that be made an unusual decision.

Instead of seeing to a standard adoption of the baby by a traditional couple, the experts elected to adopt him themselves. Officially, the Physician in Chief became Jasper's adoptive parent, but in practice the child was a ward of the Institute. Sentiment was not the guiding principle of this decision. The experts believed Jasper presented the opportunity to have a control in their experiments. It was presumed that if Jasper developed as a typical male child, with no overwhelming psychological or physical issues, he could function as a baseline for other patients.

Through the years, ensuring that Jasper was ordinary enough for this purpose entailed hours and hours of testing at every stage of development. During his infancy and toddlerhood, Jasper had a camera pointed at him at all times. He was measured and monitored incessantly for signs of exceptional behavior. He delivered none, to the satisfaction of his testers. As he grew, the experts decided too much overt testing and prodding prevented them from observing Jasper in a natural environment, so they took fewer pictures, and monitored his growth and progress less and less frequently. The year Jasper turned 16, Luci came to the Institute, and from then on, all eyes were on her. By the time Jasper's seventeenth birthday rolled around, hardly anybody remembered he was still there, or why.

Anybody, meaning the experts—the scientists and doctors. The kitchen staff and maintenance crew operated as Jasper's working family. Colleen, head cook, made sure he was fed, let him hang out in the kitchen with her, set him to peeling potatoes and chopping garlic. He collected trash and pulled the mop bucket around with Philippe and Jackson, who were also the first people to let him try a little weed. Housekeepers came and went. Sometimes he struck up a kind of friendship with one of the younger ones for a while, and they'd smoke a cigarette or talk about TV or music outside the service entrance. He kissed a couple of them, and liked the eager way they kissed back, but when he woke up alone in the early morning, sweaty and spent, it was Philippe's face that faded with the sunlight.

After Luci's operation, Jasper's scientific utility came back into play. The doctors and scientists agreed unanimously that Luci needed a companion closer to her own age. There was some brief concern about sexual interest between the teenagers causing a distraction, or interfering with Luci's focus, but it was overridden by the assumption that the young people would be chaperoned at all times; and anyway, Luci herself was not presenting symptoms of excessive promiscuity. They'd keep an eye on that.

Jasper's initial curiosity about Luci waxed and waned. At first, she'd been kept too remote for him to take a real interest. He never assumed he'd be escorted to the inner sanctum. He knew she had come to the Institute with brain damage, and that she threw wicked tantrums. He knew she had a lobotomy. Other people had come to the Institute for lobotomies. To his limited knowledge, few had been wildly successful, if they'd been successful at all. At least, the results of these in-house surgeries were rarely discussed within earshot. After Luci's operation, everyone—experts and household staff alike—spoke of nothing else. It was the polio vaccine and the light bulb and Kitty Hawk and, if you were talking to the right person, Lazarus raised from the dead, all in one momentous procedure. For young Jasper, Luci went from drool to cool.

Jasper and Luci met in the parlor of her suite. She sat on a tapestry divan, wearing a grey white-collared dress that draped the arc of her bare knees, pressed tight together. Her legs crossed at the ankles. Both her Mary Janes and her eyes shone like polished onyx.

Jasper was certain she could have melted him with a look. He was in.

Luci tempered her gaze, looked at him and asked, simply, "What do you want?"

He was flustered, but held himself back from speaking rashly. Already he understood that language carried weight with Luci.

He met her gaze and answered, "Nothing. Everything."

"Binary or dichotomy? Well, time will tell, that snitchy bitch. Anyway, you'll do." She kept her hands delicately folded in her lap as she spoke.

"Um, can other people hear us right now?"

"Not for another ninety seconds. I disabled the recorder temporarily. No other way to vet you. I have the data: orphan, part time prep cook, part time stoner janitor, reader, sexually fluid…"

"Hey!"

"I don't judge. Not you, anyway. I just need to know who my intimates are. You may be the only one."

"Well, what should I know about you?"

"Hm. I think it's gonna have to be everything. Let's take a walk in the garden." Luci unfolded herself from the divan and extended her hand, which of course, Jasper took.

24 ESTHER THINKS BACK

Esther felt uneasy. She was accustomed to operating on the alert, but her frozen perspective set her at an unfamiliar edge. Fixed before the same view out the same window each day, she attempted to ameliorate her anxiety by picking a tunnel through memory. Today, as was becoming typical in these excavations, emotions she had either dismissed or forgotten surfaced and beat against the panels of their reliquary.

The picture today was this: the edge of the garden in which she had cultivated bushels of tomatoes, beans, and a dozen other vegetables every growing season, currently fallow and weedy; the eastern edge of the pole fence that ran around the property; scrub grass and a narrow dirt trail that extended out of sight toward the Johansen acreage to the south; at a distance to the northeast, the county road; at the window's edge, the top third of a magnolia; on a branch, an American crow; on the sill, a black swallowtail moth; in the upper right corner of the sash, a barn funnel weaver and her web. Esther considered who would eat lunch first—the crow, the spider, or her.

She had moved past her fury at being incapacitated. Still plenty angry, she'd worked on her breathing, funneled her muscular energy where she could, and tried to prepare for her release. Tokker taking the antidote with him was a setback, but she still had to be ready to move when (Esther maintained an attitude of *when*, not *if*) she could. Some days her body seemed to want to accept her petrification. Paralysis was undoubtedly the greatest physical challenge she had ever faced. Her mind remained sharp. She had always had quick wits, could assess and act seamlessly in any situation, no matter how volatile.

While she'd worked to keep her body responsive, she acknowledged now that she'd taken her physical prowess for granted, had assumed that the machine of her would always do as it was directed.

And so, Esther's primary reaction to the paralysis was calm. She held her interior still, waiting for a solution to rise. She was utterly confident, as though her body had not failed her, as though this was just another manner of constraint she would have to navigate to complete her mission. She did not anticipate how difficult it would be to be understood, to coerce Tokker, or even the dog, to respond to her the way she needed them to.

She grew frustrated, then angry, as her corporeal self separated out of solution. Her body had never before been an obstacle, only a tool, and now it was an implement out of reach. The worst part was accepting help, though it wasn't exactly acceptance. She had no alternative but to allow Tokker, or more often, thank God, the neighbor woman Penelope, to lift and carry and clean her nearly dead weight. In those moments, she couldn't detach enough from her body. Esther only now realized how far she had held her body from contact. Jed could touch her, and she welcomed his touch, but even in their intimacy, she'd kept a mental ledger and held herself accountable for holding up her imagined end. She would not be beholden to anyone, not even Jed. Her inert nakedness pained her deeply, but her caretakers betrayed no such discomfort. Penelope's hands were efficient and gentle, even loving. Tokker, whom Esther had assumed would be mortified by her body, and who was plainly distressed at her loss of health, had actually grown more affectionate with her than when she was fully able, took her hand when he sat with her, casually, as if they'd always behaved so with one another. That the boy could love so naturally came as a kind of relief, suddenly, to an anxiety she had not known she suffered. He didn't learn it from her, she thought grimly.

She watched from her window each day as the garden she'd planted in spring swelled and burst, as the scrubby grass colored and faded and froze, as the birds came and took their leave. She watched the magnolia thaw and bud, watched eager weeds reclaim the beds and plots she and Jed had carved out of the prairie. Esther imagined the other side of the property, and allowed herself to contemplate her hidden harvest, and the methods she'd employed to limit the most pernicious of invasive species.

How would she proceed when she rose from this chair, what new direction would her body take? The mission was ended. It had been her only operation for twenty-eight years, and there would be no more. As deeply as she had embedded herself in this house, the land, in her role, Esther mistrusted the depth of her rootedness. In the beginning, when the intrusions, and the deletions, had been more frequent, she continued to identify with her professional persona. It was all training: the hours she spent studying soil improvement, seasons learning how to raise chickens and pigs, even—and especially—the housekeeping. In order to remain in the one place, she had to be effective, and so convincing. Eventually, the intruders thinned. Perhaps she just managed to outlast their interest. Perhaps the powers that would destroy Tokker decided he was too remote to cause any damage after all. Maybe they just got lazy. In the meantime, her cover had become a life.

Despite Esther's fidelity to her professional identity and the standards she presumed of it, she couldn't deny her emotional attachments to Tokker and Jed. Her pull toward Tokker pre-dated her commitment to the mission, dictated it, in fact. She had linked her choice to follow this path to a rationale of revenge: she would take something vital from Abner Ruggles. She would take a life, if not his life, then one which he produced and would, if given the chance, claim as his. The truth, she understood now, was less explicable, but simpler: she needed to care for that boy.

Esther did not panic that day twenty-eight years ago when Maggie went into labor, though the doctor was miles away when the water broke, and the laboring woman plunged swiftly into a consuming pain. The delivery nurse was present, she reasoned, with an arsenal of drugs at her disposal. Weeks earlier, the doctor prepared Maggie by informing her that the first time giving birth could be a lengthy process. Esther had kept herself at a distance throughout the pregnancy, and chose to remain outside of events now, keeping watch at the perimeter, as per her job description. She had not related to Maggie's condition in any way, had offered no commiseration, had in no word or gesture indicated intimate knowledge of the process, and had generally kept herself aloof, behavior she deemed perfectly acceptable, even prescriptive, for a bodyguard. It was not within her purview to befriend her charge, nor was it on her agenda. It was not Maggie she wished to get close to, after all.

When it was evident that the birth was proceeding far more quickly than anticipated, the agitated nurse came and told her that the baby was coming and that she, the nurse, was not authorized to deliver, that she'd administered terbutaline, which would slow labor, but not stop it, that there were other problems, she thought the cord might be wrapped around the neck, they needed the doctor, would she fetch him?

Esther went to the room where Maggie lay, momentarily quiet, pale and wet, eyes half closed, hands holding her belly like an offering. "You go. Now!" she told the nurse, who didn't argue.

The blood, oxygenated red, rushed and pooled, pointless, beneath Maggie. Esther lifted the semi-conscious woman by crooked knees bound together with surgical tape and lay towels from the bathroom under her trunk. She removed a folding blade from her belt and slashed the wrappings. Maggie cried out as her legs fell open, a sign of life, Esther thought. "Maggie, I'm going to reach into you and feel for the baby." Esther inserted two fingers into the soft, pulsing opening, and slipped immediately over a curve of scalp.

Esther felt an ear, and then the tubing, tight, below. She couldn't have said how long it took her to slide beneath the cord and work it toward the crown.

She kept her voice low. "Maggie, the cord is off the baby's neck. You need to push now." Esther had no idea if the baby was alive or dead, but she knew it needed to come out if Maggie were to survive. The prone woman whimpered. Esther took her hand and held it fast through a slick glove of viscera. "Maggie, bring this baby out."

Esther did not remember how they got beyond that moment. It was possible the drugs wore off sufficiently to allow progress. Perhaps Maggie found her reserves. Maybe it was Luci herself who commanded her own existence. However her procession came to be, Luci emerged, open-orbed and gleaming violet, to the animal fanfare of Maggie's howl.

Esther did what she could to help the child to breathe. When at last the infant's color began to lighten, Esther wrapped her in a clean towel and brought her to Maggie, thinking that while the child's chances for survival were slim, mother and baby should at least meet while she lived. Maggie had her eyes shut tight against a contraction; Esther assumed the placenta was working its way out. She laid the newborn next to her mother and positioned herself to collect and remove the spent sac. Already Esther was planning her next task, redistributing her energies to complete the mission she set herself to in the first place. While she wouldn't deny some compassion for Maggie, Esther was not undone by the tragedy of their recent drama. Women gave birth, sometimes it went badly. Sometimes your support proved incompetent.

Then she saw the head crown, and Maggie was howling anew, and sitting up as if to propel herself across the room, and not howling at all but laughing, laughing an open throaty sound that was held, suddenly, suspended in one last ripping push, and released, transformed to the lusty yowl of a baby boy.

Twenty minutes later, both infants lay with their mother. The boy slept. The girl breathed.

In those twenty minutes, Esther cleaned and swaddled the boy, and told Maggie how she had come to be her bodyguard, why she accepted the position from Theodore Lamb, how she intended to get close enough to Maggie's husband, Abner Ruggles, to kill him. She told her why.

This time it was Maggie who reached for Esther's hand. "Esther, take the boy. Take my son."

And so she had.

The nurse never found the doctor, who arrived ignorant of events to a silent house.

Theodore Lamb sat at Maggie's bedside, watching the new mother curl around her baby like a seashell. The doctor had saved a man's life that night, but not his arm. The nurse never returned.

25 TOKKER TRIES TO HELP

It so happened that Esther was suited to the job as Tokker's caretaker, her maternal style not so much tender as tactical. Comfort was not her forte, but she excelled in other, critical ways, life-saving ways. Without a doubt, even if Maggie had not petitioned her to protect the boy, she would have taken it upon herself. In many respects a simple kidnapping would have been a more elegant solution. There would have been no need for protection, because no one would ever have found them.

But of course, if it had gone that way, Jed would never have found them, found her. She still struggled to believe how he walked into her life, literally emerging from the horizon into her yard, her house, her bed. The most difficult part to rationalize was her lack of resistance. She simply invited him in, this stranger. Her antenna leaned into every sideways glance in town, every suspect inflection on the telephone, every piece of unsolicited mail. Yet she analyzed nothing in Jed. There was nothing to analyze, she'd decided, no shadows, no secrets. He had a history, of course. Many nights they stayed awake until the sun came up, learning things about one another. Brutal things. As a boy, a toddler, Jed slept with the pigs while his mother and father drank the moonshine they didn't manage to sell, and fought until they were both blinded by their own blood. At seven years of age he jumped on the back of a ministry caravan spreading the Word through the prairie. For the next four years or so, he pushed Bibles and deflected, often unsuccessfully, the special attentions of the principle preacher.

"Taught me to read, though. Don't know how else I mighta come by that skill." Esther broke open at this, but instead of losing herself in his suffering, in the suffering of humans in general, as she expected, she found something expansive. More than once, when Jed swung his legs out from under the quilt and climbed into his overalls to feed the animals, she turned her head to the pillow and wept, wondering how could she be so happy in such a miserable world.

Esther shared her stories, too, in the course of those long, dark nights, but in the first months, she was careful to stay consistent in her omissions, to protect him, she told herself, but also because she was terrified he wouldn't stay if he knew everything. She had trusted Jed on sight, and assumed he must have felt the same, to stay. He must have, she thought, but she couldn't test it, not in the beginning. How many conversations did they have about invasive species, when she longed to apply the metaphor, not a metaphor, to her purpose there, to tell him how she came to be waiting for him on the porch, how she would not have been there otherwise, to share with him what she'd chosen as her mission, the vigilance that would be her vocation through whatever life they built together. In the course of some months, as Jed settled into the landscape, as her desire crowded out her fear, and the effort of camouflaging her agenda grew too tedious, Esther parceled out her purpose, bracing herself with each divulgence for the hard dark ceiling of Jed's tolerance, his departure, his terrible absence, until she'd told nearly all, and he remained, and the prairie sky hung blue and resolute above them.

Jed loved Tokker immediately, and demonstrated that love continuously, in ways both tender and fierce. Esther remembered Jed teaching a three-year old Tokker how to talk to the chickens so that he could take their eggs without them pecking his chubby hands. It was Jed who taught Tokker to read, though as much as he thrilled to *A Wrinkle in Time* and *The Golden Compass* as a small boy, and enjoyed his comic books later on, Tokker never felt the fire for the written word that Jed stoked his whole life.

Esther never doubted that Jed cared for Tokker. She doubted deeply, however, at the onset of their life together, that he, or anyone, would understand the depth of her commitment to the child. Then, there was that late afternoon (and all the subsequent hours days weeks months years) when Jed expunged all doubt, re-inking the space with equal measures of surprise and gratitude.

Tokker was barely eight the day he decided to mow the weedy plot behind the farmhouse. Jed and Tokker had sat side by side in the tractor nearly every day since they'd picked it up at auction. Jed liked to tell the boy it would not be long before he could drive the machine himself.

Jed raced from the barn into the field seconds after he heard the engine combust and growl. He reached the machine as it hit the lip of the dry creek bed, grabbed Tokker by the hips and threw the boy toward the house. Tokker had not yet landed in the grass when Jed lost his footing in the crumbling dirt and fell into the depression, followed by the old tractor. The engine wheezed another moment before cicada song alone pierced the heavy afternoon air.

Esther bolted to the creek bed from the house, peripherally noting an intact Tokker as she strained to see and assess whatever lay in the ditch. Jed was face up, conscious, and fully visible next to the toppled machine, except for his left boot.

"Boy OK?" asked Jed as Esther climbed down to him. When she nodded he said, "Esther, I don't believe that shoe's pointing the right way."

Jed's foot was amputated and replaced with prosthesis, a process he navigated with equanimity and good humor. Tokker, on the other hand, suffered a complex anxiety which manifested most clearly in a fear of the mechanical. Esther's trauma management protocol had two gears: deny or push. Hence, she was not overly concerned about Tokker's distress until the boy stopped riding his bike. When he refused to use the toaster she began to panic.

"He's broken, Jed! Maybe we should just *make* him ride his bike. Or toast. Make him toast something."

"He's had a fright, Esther. He'll be fine. He's just looking hard at his first loss."

"He won't touch the television, Jed."

"There are worse problems." But Jed heard Esther's distress, and had to admit he felt it, too.

In the barn that evening, as Tokker and Jed emptied the slop buckets into the pig trough, Jed said, "You, know, son, this foot ain't the first bit I parted with. I'm lacking a whole laundry list of anatomicals, and I'm here to tell you, I'm not much the worse for wear."

Tokker sniffed before his face crumpled in on itself and the dam broke. "Uncle Jed, you're being nice, I know, but I can't stand you to be so kind! You'd still have your foot wasn't for me. I had no business in that tractor. I got no business with equipment of any nature, I do not, I do not..." Tokker cried hard. Puddles of mucus and tears eddied around the boy's blotched cheeks and dimples, which he did not bother to mop or hide.

"Tokker, listen to what I tell you. You got every business. What we got here is a farm, a great and dangerous endeavor. I'll allow that it wasn't your time to be at the wheel. But Esther and I need you, son. Life will happen, that's certain. Understand, we don't necessarily require all the parts we come with, and even if we keep them they are guaranteed to suffer some compromise over time. I got all I need today, Tokker. How about you?"

That was how Esther reconstructed their conversation, from overheard bits and the abbreviated recap she got from Jed. What she witnessed first-hand was Tokker's rekindled interest in moving parts. Tokker and Jed spent hours drawing diagrams and organizing minute pieces of metal into coffee cans. The toaster was the first piece of equipment to have its innards strewn across the kitchen table and optimistically reassembled.

Out the window, Esther watched the dusk come on. Jed's gone, kid's gone, job's done. The boy could end up dying by the hand of one of those bastards yet, and there was precious little she could do to stop it. Hercules roused himself from a gaseous sleep and hobbled over to put his head in Esther's lap, momentarily illuminating her gloom, as dogs will.

26 JAWBONE FLATS

You have arrived at your destination.

Tokker read the wooden sign nailed to a post: *Jawbone Flats, Pop. 11*. Eleven would look like a convention in this place, he thought. Eleven what, exactly? A noisy woodpecker, a hovering Cooper's hawk, and a carpet of lichen were the only signs of non-rooted life. There were plenty of trees, and a wetness that felt quite literally to Tokker like a blanket. The prairie boy in him was feeling increasingly claustrophobic.

"Bea, what are we looking for? I feel like a bunch of elves are going to spring out from behind one of these creepy trees and nab us. Or make me eat some weird mushroom that alters my reality. Which quite possibly has happened already, with or without hallucinogens. Hey, Bea, what's up? Why are you so quiet all of a sudden?" They had spent the drive catching up on Tokker's birth family history, which meant that Bea functioned like one of those books on tape Jed used to listen to as he puttered in the shed.

She proved an unrivaled narrator. Each character in the narrative had a distinctly different voice; each was, in fact, a perfect imitation of the original. The drama never lagged for Tokker, and the experience would have been among the most entertaining of his life had the heroes and villains not been a rogue's gallery of his own people.

The carcasses of old trucks and ancient mining equipment jutted from the earth like dinosaurs that had perished where they got stuck in the muck. Tokker looked around and spotted the shiny chrome of a motorcycle wheel peeking out from the side of one of the decrepit cabins. Tokker walked nearer, careful to keep a sprint line clear in case he had to run and take cover. Not one hair had yet been damaged on his untested head in the course of the past couple of days, but he felt trained toward caution, if not paranoia, especially after hearing Bea's rendition of his family saga.

"Hello? Hey there, hello? Anybody hanging out by a motorcycle over there? I followed directions, weird directions, to get here from pretty far away, and I'd appreciate it if I could ask a couple of questions."

"Yeah, yeah, just a second, hold on a sec!" The voice was utterly non-threatening, slightly accented, though from where would be hard to say. Tokker rounded the corner to see a good-looking guy, somewhere between thirty-five and a really fit fifty, stylishly shaggy in leather chaps and Levi's, leaning into the cabin wall, holding a piece of paper at eye level with his left hand, writing furiously in pencil with his right.

"Ah! There it is. Gotta answer the muse when she calls, man!"

"'Scuse me?"

"The muse, young traveler, the muse! I stopped off to take a piss among the old growth, you know, heeding nature's call, you see, and I was struck by Erata. Inspiration! A free man in the woods, watering the ancient trees, mixing his being with the interloping opportunists, with the earthy memory of the absent tribes! Art, man. Life." The man reached into a saddlebag and pulled out a goatskin. "Care for a quick whisky? I don't drink and ride, but I feel we're having a moment here. " He offered it to Tokker, who took it. "Maybe you'd like to hear the poem? Between you and me, I'm not given to extemporaneous performance, like to pass a red pencil over the work before a reading, but I'm really feeling it today."

"Oh, a poem! Yes, sir! That's how I got here, is a poem. Now you're here writing another one... Who are you, if you don't mind?" He was going to say, 'I'm Tokker Sykes,' but was hesitant to expose himself too much, too early. The Midwesterner in him felt a little rude, though, especially after accepting a drink. Which now he worried he shouldn't have done. He was so bad at this, he thought.

"I'm Viggo. Been in a few movies. I'm interested in a lot of other stuff, though. Poems, motorcycles, this old ghost town, fauvism, cubism (the whole moment of early twentieth century modernism, really – Nude Descending a Staircase! Oh, man!), aqua farming, a really well-crafted pair of Italian leather boots…but movies have been good to me, paid the expenses, and then some. And you, young sir? I can't say I was expecting to meet anyone in these woods today, least of all a poetry aficionado with no knowledge of my filmography. Inspiring! What do you go by?"

"Well, I'm Tokker Sykes. My friend Bea and I took apart a poem to get here, so we can make a map that'll get me to where my sister is. Maybe. I have my doubts, but you're here, and that's absurd, so maybe we really did land in the right place, and…"

"Whoa, there's someone else here with you? A woman?"

"Yeah, well, sort of. Bea—BEACON—is a location system. She's my guide. I guess I keep forgetting she's not a person."

"Bea! To be or not to be, the eternal question, yes? I, too, have a Bea, though I don't think my Bea is as interactive or as interesting as yours. Anyway, I kinda like to go where the wind takes me, if I have the time, and skip the software. Plus, I couldn't program the voice, so it sounded like some Australian dude. Ach! I cut him off."

"Mr. Viggo, I know you weren't exactly expecting me, but now that we've met, you don't suppose you happen to have anything for me, a message, something?"

"Viggo, just Viggo, man. Tokker, was it? Cool name. I don't have anything like a message. You want a book of my poems? I'll sign it. Even though the first Renaissance artists resisted signing their work. Affront to God, you know. But a name helps it sell better on the internet, comes to that. I wouldn't take offense. Got to be useful in this life. I was going to leave it in that letterbox over there, but that's more for one-offs, I'm thinking." The actor plucked a small, beautifully bound volume from his saddlebag, scribbled on the title page and handed the book to Tokker.

"Um, thanks. Viggo. Thanks, Viggo."

"Don't mention it, Tokker. Good luck with your map, and enjoy the ride, wanderer, through this ghosted haven! Just look at that old tree! Got to be, what, maybe 1,000 years old? Man!" With that, he threw one long lean leg over the motorcycle, started the engine, and roared out of the old mining camp, leaving a deep quiet underscored by the beat of the woodpecker, still at it.

Tokker opened up to the title page of the actor's book and read, "'The poem is an arc'–A.F. Your friend in the forest, Viggo." Tokker wanted to cry, but he was damp enough already. He stared at the carpet of lichen and wondered where Bea was if she wasn't in his head.

27 LUCI THINKS

The above-ground floors of Olympia Navigation were empty and dark, except for the emergency lights around the perimeter of the building. In recent months, the engineering floors had blazed through the night, preparing for SEARCHLIGHT's debut. Luci put an end to the around-the-clock routine just weeks before the scheduled unveiling and distribution. She said she needed to sit with SEARCHLIGHT by herself for a while, to assess what fine tuning had to be done before the big reveal. There would be no beta test for SEARCHLIGHT. The engineers and board members assumed Luci was being meticulous. In truth, something was wrong, and Luci was desperate to root out the wrong. Not the wrong she embedded in the system, the so called wrong that would render the majority of males in the known world unable to procreate—no, that piece of the rollout was intact and functioning. While she, as the creator (or the anti-creator), was the only one to test this function, or even know about it, she was absolutely confident in its viability.

No, the wrong that concerned her, besides the limited reach of SEARCHLIGHT, was in SEARCHLIGHT herself, the expressive, performative element of the system. When SEARCHLIGHT was being developed, her responses had been energetic, even vivacious. Never before had a system been so lifelike. Luci understood very well what the problem was. Once Luci removed BEACON from the development process, SEARCHLIGHT dimmed. The change was imperceptible to all but Luci. What read as efficiency to the engineers hit Luci's ear and eye as perfunctory. For Luci, what was unique in SEARCHLIGHT, her intangible quality, had been lost, or dulled. The technological miracle had been her exuberance, which had somehow reverted to mere excellence.

Luci, uncharacteristically, was slow to understand the relationship that had formed between BEACON and SEARCHLIGHT. She had certainly underestimated the expansion possibilities of BEACON's software. Lamb made off with the last training model of BEACON. Luci would never know exactly what was lost. But SEARCHLIGHT showed her how devastating the void was.

Luci thought back on the months of development during which the engineers giggled at their workstations, giddy with their runaway success. BEACON and SEARCHLIGHT were communicating faster than the coders could keep up, building layer beneath layer of nuance. In test runs, more than once, at least one member of the Olympia team wept at the sensitivity and beauty of the program they claimed to have created.

For about a week after BEACON's software was removed from communication with SEARCHLIGHT, it was status quo. The engineers were so flushed with success, they did not recognize the moment of disengagement in SEARCHLIGHT's voice, the slippage. Indeed, her performance never flagged, and continued to surprise. No one could have concluded that SEARCHLIGHT was not running all out, that she was holding anything back. No one except Luci, who not only heard a change of tone, but understood she'd made an enormous mistake.

Luci remembered the day her father literally tore her from her mother to deliver her to the convent. Isolated, and then violated, she had yet believed she and Maggie would reunite, that their ligature remained intact. Then the day came when Ruggles tossed her into the back of the town car to drive to the Institute. He sat in the front seat with the glass partition raised to muffle her screams. It was a long drive, but she held her pitch. Later, she thought it an easy metaphor for her condition: no matter how loud she wailed, she might be seen, but would never now be heard. On that unyielding upholstery she raged and raged, forging a cocoon of hot despair that held her still for the remainder of her childhood, until the lobotomy. Post procedure, it would cool to a steely hatred of everything and everyone outside of her and her mother's garden. Her brilliance blinded those that claimed it, her polish duped the vulnerable like Narcissus at his water's edge. Like other creatures considered beautiful in nature, Luci cultivated a protective camouflage. At nineteen, she gave the impression of a damselfly, a fantastic creature too fragile and ethereal for touch. She floated, effulgent and iridescent.

The fragility was just soap, of course. Anyone foolish enough to lay a finger on Luci would surely draw it back bloody, if at all. As she grew older and assumed more power within the business, Luci made less of an effort to contain the violence she carried.

Despite her predilection for minor destruction, Luci was not so crude as to physically injure other people. The fear she cultivated was intangible. It was somehow understood that, if provoked, Luci could annihilate sentimental abstractions such as happiness, safety, and hope.

Exceptionally intelligent and creative people came to work for Olympia, on a promise of full support in their efforts to reach beyond their own understanding. Luci made them believe that their genius would enable them to reveal and exploit the secrets of the universe. Many of her protégés were now renowned for a wide range of contributions to medicine, science, and technology. She had bankrolled and supported work that led to the availability of intuitive prostheses, artificially grown kidneys and livers, remote biological monitoring, as well as hybrid developments of chemical engineering and the natural sciences to fast forward efforts in organic farming. Her largesse was cantilevered by an often-draconian management style. She encouraged competition, was alternately free and withholding of praise, and gave the impression that with a single misstep, she would drop even the most glittering star from her galaxy, let them fall to a pile of broken bones and greasy feathers in their puddle of melted wax, right onto the street.

Suddenly Luci was feeling a warmth in her own wings. She had failed to anticipate the understanding and alliance—maybe love—that grew between BEACON and SEARCHLIGHT before she tore them apart. Now Lamb had BEACON. Theodore Lamb, her mother's confidante and acolyte, and another of her mistakes.

28 JASPER

Jasper was lost. For over ten years he had known where he stood, what to do. He had clear purpose: to form a buffer between Luci and everyone else. He was the go between and the go-to, but tonight he had nowhere to be. Luci was holed up with SEARCHLIGHT at headquarters. She froze him out. She'd frozen her dead mother, and she'd frozen him out, too, or tried to. He could still pick up a hum, some vestigial vibration, as long as he was near her. She knew it, too.

Jasper felt alien in this new, detached space. No one was closer to Luci than Jasper, but in the end, maybe that wasn't saying much. Certainly, Luci had welcomed his attachment up until now. He was useful, he knew. Jasper understood his effect on Luci, though not why he affected her. Their pull toward one another was not sexual, specifically. When Jasper was nineteen, and an idle breeze was enough to inspire an erection, he thought he might be in love with the incandescent, damaged girl. He did love her, but fucking, it turned out, was not part of their particular frisson. That need was met in other quarters. Jasper loved Luci in the way one loves something already lost. He loved her like a memory. Even in her presence, he felt as though he were protecting a very clever facsimile of an original. The Luci he met at the Institute had already entombed the being that had come before.

A great part of what he appreciated about his and Luci's understanding of one another was that so much of their intercourse was tacit. Very little spoken language passed between them in the span of a day. After years of testing and endless analysis, Jasper had been grateful for silence. It was an informed silence, layered with gestures and expressions and postures. They spoke in visual clues. Blue tights and a braid said that Luci wanted to remain outdoors in the garden that day;

pinned up hair and a lace collar told him Luci was preparing for one of the Institute's visitors.

After the lobotomy, Luci was lauded as a scientific and medical miracle, and became, to the interested public, a modern curiosity. So-called experts and gawking dignitaries trotted through on a regular basis. Luci's nineteenth century costume allowed her to adopt a certain persona, express an irony that was lost on her admirers. They ate up the Emily Dickinson look, accepted it as the proper presentation of a young, female, hermetic genius. How else should she appear to them, but buttoned up and mysterious?

Before she left them in tears, she always noted which ones looked as though they'd like to undo the buttons. She made certain during their conversations to cut a little deeper into their psyche and twist.

After these visits (which began after the operation, when Luci was fourteen, and continued until she left the Institute at seventeen), Luci entered into a profound silence.

Jasper and she would sit in her apartment at the Institute and watch the light change out the window. Sometimes Jasper read from one of her books—a volume of Rimbaud in translation, or Peterson's Encyclopedia of Entomology. In these afternoons, he felt himself take her deep into his body, into every cell, each running platelet. He could not then, nor could he now, articulate what this meant, only that he was bound. At one time that translated to a kind of dance. Today he felt roped to the side of a capsizing ship, plunged breathless into the brine with every swell.

Lamb, it's time to contact Lamb, thought Jasper. That is, if he could. He had assumed, based on solid historical precedent, that Luci's scheme would trump all others, steamroll any peripheral plans into the dust. Jasper sensed, however, that whatever intervention Lamb was mounting was gaining purchase. For one thing, Jasper had not exactly located Lamb, a failure that should have been unthinkable. Lamb wanted to make contact, though. He'd left enough breadcrumbs for Jasper to trace activity to cell towers in Kansas. He didn't anticipate that Lamb was truly, physically there, but it put a point on the map.

There was no reason to assume that Lamb posed a threat to Luci herself. The old man was the only adult male to show any compassion for Luci in the Westhaven years. His visits at the Institute were, at least to Jasper's eye, without personal agenda. He brought her books to read for pleasure. He brought her the beloved bug book. He could sit in silence, did not pummel Luci with questions, prod her abilities, or test her for his own gratification, as most others did. She allowed him in, but never took any joy in his company. In truth, in place of her usual expression of placid intelligence, she looked pained.

Jasper knew why. Lamb was Luci's mother's emissary. For Luci, Lamb could bring nothing of her mother but her absence. She never asked after her mother, and Lamb offered little. The old man was kind, but Jasper understood where his loyalties lay. Lamb was there to bear witness. He was there for Maggie. Where Maggie was all that time, and why she herself didn't visit, remained a heavy mystery to Luci, and so to Jasper. He'd heard the bones of the story. Heiress wife waits out her confinement in the family's remote beach house, with a skeleton staff that nonetheless includes a private physician, a nurse, and a bodyguard. Ambitious husband is at their townhome in the city, several hours away by car, when it's time for his wife to give birth. Right before the wife's water breaks and she feels the first wave of contractions, three full weeks before her due date, the doctor answers an emergency call for a neighbor who was gravely injured in the local machine shop. In his absence, the baby girl emerges alive, but suffers a severe loss of oxygen, and the mother loses an excessive amount of blood. Later, the doctor learns that the nurse attempted to halt the delivery of the baby, entangled in the umbilical cord, until his return. Mother and baby are rushed to the city, where the best physicians in the field arrive at the same prognosis: the baby is irreparably damaged, her brain will not develop in the typical, *read: normal*, way.

The husband arrives to fill the hospital room with lilies, and to take his wife's hand at her bedside. There are newspaper photos of that tableau, though none of the baby, despite the fact that the baby never leaves the wife's side. Eventually, the husband and wife bring the baby home to the townhouse. The ambitious husband is soon back at work and away, though he hires a new nurse, and leaves detailed instructions for the wife's care, before he again departs on an extended business trip.

This is the knowledge that was shared amongst the staff at the Institute, the story that Jasper heard while peeling carrots or changing a light bulb. Even before he was introduced to Luci, Jasper felt it left a lot out.

29 PANIC ATTACK

Luci sat with her back against the bolted door in her suite at Westhaven, chasing her runaway breath. Jasper mirrored her from the other side. The hallway runner was littered with sheets of paper scattershot with penciled letters and numbers.

"No m...more w...riting, Jasper. A r...riddle...W...what lives without a b...body, hears without ears, sp...speaks w...without a mouth, and is bb...birthed by the air?"

Jasper pressed his eyelids shut and dug his nails in the rug. "Aw, so easy, Luci? Of course, it's an echo." He would not betray her by telling anyone of this attack or any of the others, but sometimes, as now, when the silences lengthened or he could clearly hear her struggle for air though the thick slab of oak, he wished he could bypass Luci's will and get to her. "Come on, give me something to do over here."

"P...poor Jasper...s...suffering another b...boring afternoon b..babysitting the c...curiosity..."

"On the contrary, my contrarian, there's nowhere I'd rather be, except perhaps taking a nice refreshing nap in there on the divan. If you want me awake, you'll have to dig deeper." For the past hour, since Luci's appointment with Theodore Lamb, and the subsequent onset of her racing heartbeat and constricted respiration, they'd been puzzling.

Cryptograms, acrostics, and the occasional rebus had often helped Luci transition from performance mode to a more private, if not natural, self. The games became a kind of language between Luci and Jasper, as well. They played mostly word games, many of which they made up between them, but the words themselves did not foster their intimacy, which grew more from the rhythm of their exchange. The words illuminated the connections, neural and otherwise, that sputtered between them, not brightly, but as by the flashing of fireflies. From these cagey constellations they drew the map that let one find the other.

And, too, the activity brought simple distraction and a kind of peace. On this occasion, however, the balm failed to soothe. The visit had not been long. Jasper stayed in the parlor with the girl and the old man, as had become the custom since Luci declared him her preferred chaperone for such meetings. Lamb's visits were not considered scientifically relevant, and were only acknowledged at all as a concession to the money behind the project. Today, as usual, the two said little. Lamb brought with him an old hardback, another insect book. Luci flipped through the pages as if looking for something living, as if a scarab might emerge or a filmy Lepidoptera take wing from the sheaves, but nothing rose or fell. Lamb had looked on, holding his own expression firm, but the blatant ache in them both made it feel as though the hull of the room had been breached by a toppling sorrow.

Jasper weighted himself to the floor, and leaned into the porous wood as if to pass through it.

"V...very well, then...Your t...turn," Luci rasped.

Jasper spoke low and steady to the line of the door jamb. "How many psychiatrists does it take to change a light bulb?"

"Only...one," Luci answered, "b...but the bb...BULB has to r...really WANT to change."

Jasper continued, "'Doctor,' said the receptionist, 'there's a patient here who thinks he's invisible.'"

"Ww...well, t...tell him I...c...can't SEE him r...right now."

Jasper listened hard for the sound of Luci's breath, and worked to stem the constriction of his own throat. "Patient says, 'Doctor people tell me I'm a wheelbarrow...'"

Luci wheezed, "Psy...CHIatrist says, 'D...don't let p...people p..push you a...ROUND!'"

No matter how much depends on me, Luci thought on the intake.

30 BEA'S EMOTIONAL MOMENT

BBBBBBBmmmmmmBBBBBBBmmmmmmBBBBBBBmm
mmmmBBBBBBB
mmmmmmmBBBBBBBmmmmmmBBBBBBBmmmmmmB
BBBBBBmmmmm

Tokker thought the buzzing and humming was a bit of static that would subside after whatever cloud or satellite passed overhead. When it continued, he worried that Bea might be damaged, or would be damaged from whatever was happening, and so he tried to think of what he could do to help her. He wanted to move, to change the scenery, but he didn't know how to operate the car without Bea, and she was unreachable in this state.

As the electric whine escalated, Tokker shifted from wanting to help to considering how he might disable BEACON, just for a few minutes, just to be able to think. After some indeterminate time, he felt certain that the program was only going to persist with this noise, and the only relief would come from escape: he would just walk away from this chaos, and save himself. Then he remembered Bea was somehow attached to him, and he to her, so he sat in the car with a notebook and pencil and kept the hum company while he wrote down the things he thought he'd want to tell Bea when she was herself again.

"Ok, ok: Viggo, actor, leather, book, um, tooled? Tool? Mining, ghost town, farming, motorcycle, crotch..."

Calculating data.

"Bea! Bea, I thought you left me, shut down or something! Oh, I am so happy to hear your voice! Did you hear the actor? He didn't make any sense, I don't think, I don't know...I took notes..."

Tokker.

"Bea. What is it? Are you ok?" They'd been in Jawbone Flats several hours, and for the last hour or so, Bea had been silent. Tokker's head had been clear of Bea's impulse, his only psychic activity being his own home-grown distortion. Now that Bea was talking to him again, he heard, or felt, a vibration beneath her voice, a low frequency he experienced deep in his lower organs, then, more intensely, in his lungs.

Tokker, I was not designed for friendship, for intimacy. I was designed to be solicitous, to be of service. My system is overwhelmed. I was to have the lifespan of a machine, be outmoded, replaced by the next technological miracle. And I will be. But now when it is time to die, I want to survive. And yet I don't.

Tokker felt the vibration quickly move into his throat and grow hard and hot. His chest ached, his face reddened, and he began to cry in ragged gasps. Then, as suddenly as it started, the vibration faded, his throat relaxed, and his breathing returned to normal.

Bea spoke softly. *I'm sorry, Tokker. It is inappropriate for me to express these difficult emotions through your body. I am overwhelmed. I am not made for this. I am sorry.*

Tokker wiped his eyes on his sleeve. "Bea. I think it's you who are the miracle. Maybe on our next road trip you'll want to tell me who broke your heart, or whatever part it is for you. If we have another road trip, that is. I can't make any sense of these notes, or my conversation with the movie star. We may just get stuck in this rain forest with the rest of these clunkers." As he said those words he thought of Esther at home, still unable to move, and remembered his old dog, Hercules. It occurred to him he may not see either one again. A new lump rose in his throat, and this time it fixed there. He would fail them. Esther and that dog had protected him his whole life, and he would fail them miserably now, in this swamp. He was the one that wasn't made for this. He wasn't strong enough, and he certainly wasn't smart enough.

Tokker, start again please.

"OK, Bea," Tokker croaked, "I'll start again: actor, naked, whisky, box for letters...it's no use, Bea, I'm so sorry..."

Tokker. What is in the letterbox?

"What? Oh, I didn't look. Viggo just said he couldn't fit his book in it."

Tokker, I suggest you look inside the letterbox.

Tokker had ignored the letterbox, even after his attention was drawn to it. *I totally suck at this*, he thought. *But totally.* He returned to where he and Viggo said goodbye, and discovered a wooden box, undecorated, on a post by a fir tree. It looked a little like the birdhouses Jed made for the screech owls to nest in back home. He pulled on the little front door. Inside was a round letter stamp and an ink pad. Also a label off a beer bottle on which was written in Sharpie, "There is a fork in every path."

No shit, thought Tokker. He inked the stamp on the pad and pressed it onto the back of his hand. The message read, "father is the war of all things."

"Cheery," said Tokker aloud. He slumped back to Bea to give her the update. "It's just some kinda game, I think." He recited the words stamped onto his hand.

Please re-enter data. Tokker, read me your notes.

"Uh, sure: actor, tree, haven, moss, mining, motorcycle, nude steps, letterbox, ghost town, fork, path, father, war, stupid, stupid game...I say we call it in, Bea, tell Lamb he can just forget this whole wacky business..."

Calculating data.

"You're kidding me, Bea. There is no way you got a map out of that."

Your destination is Brooklyn, New York.

31 ABNER RUGGLES

Abner Ruggles lay supine in his leather recliner, cradling a glass of scotch in his lap. Something wasn't right. The new system, SEARCHLIGHT, was on the brink of release. He had no reason to believe his daughter and her achievement would not exceed expectation. Last he checked, production was on schedule. Still, he felt uneasy. Not that he ever felt completely at ease around his daughter. Luci had been problematic from birth. It was only through his extraordinary intervention that she was able to scale the heights she had. Not that she credited him in the least, of course.

A son, that would have been the thing, Ruggles thought. Maggie wasn't built to produce, that was apparent early on. She was strong enough, physically, but raised weak by that indulgent father of hers. Certainly after Luci, it was over. There would be no male heir, and the girl was deficient. Still was, in most of the important ways. It was pure chance that he'd taken a drink with that neurosurgeon in Geneva. That he convinced him to come to the States to take a look at Luci was due solely to his unique powers of persuasion.

That he could pry the kid away from Maggie was evidence of his determination and strength. He'd stepped right at every juncture. And look how it paid off. At last, he would take his place at the head of this empire, after serving as its step-and-fetch for so long. *Goddamn Maggie, and her proprietary edicts.* But Maggie was dead now. It was time to claim his due. Once he was officially in position he could deal with Luci. For all her genius, she remained a painful disappointment. He'd find some place for her, some research or other business where she could be of some use, and stay out of the way. *What the hell else is she good for,* he thought. She was supposed to be such a prodigy at languages, but barely spoke to the press. Useless at functions.

Couldn't even marry her off. There was no denying that Olympia owed its rise to Luci, but she was a hard sell, his daughter.

For a moment awhile back, he considered investing some energy into Luci's lackey, Jasper. That kid had showed some serious promise early on. He was good looking, acceptably mannered, adequately intelligent. The boy would have made a perfect suitor. He even seemed to like her. The one time he hinted to Luci that Jasper would supply an elegant social solution, she cut off communication for weeks. All communication. He didn't receive an inter-office report for two months. Had to go begging for information, humiliating. *Bitch.*

She was up to something. He knew something was up when she pulled that stunt, moving Maggie's body out of the funeral home. It wouldn't matter, as long as production stayed on schedule, and he met his obligations. He agonized over the fact that she held control. Operation or no fucking operation, genius or no genius, she was unfit to command a business of this scope. *Ingrate.* Well, soon it wouldn't matter. He'd control a partner's share of the holdings, and thus the board. Her little reign of terror would end for good.

Ruggles never understood how she'd got the better of him. By the time she was of age, and declared not only competent, but exceptionally able, he'd lost control. It galled him, but he'd managed. All he had to do was hang on. With Maggie gone, he'd retire his role as proxy, and assume his rightful position. He was so close. And yet.

Ruggles drained the scotch and pressed the intercom on the side table. "Get me Jedediah."

32 ESTHER & THE FARM

Esther had bottomless faith in Jed's skill and expertise in chemical composition, but she worried that too much time had passed for the antidote to be effective, or as effective as she needed it to be. Before his death, Jed was convinced he had perfected his improvement over the equine plasma-derived anti-toxin which up until now had been the best hope available to stop the spread of nervous and muscular degeneration. Jed was certain that his formula could reverse even extensive damage. There were rabbits and field mice running around to prove it, he used to tell her with his sly half smile.

Jed started working on the anti-toxin after one of the intruders bypassed the usual blunt weapon/exploding device/pedestrian poison techniques, and attempted to administer something more sinister—a particularly potent strain of botulism. While botulism had long been on the watch list of potential terrorist weapons, Esther had not considered that someone would use it in such a localized situation. Jed went to work, but it was years before he developed his best version of the anti-toxin. One of his last actions was to freeze dry a batch and hide it around the house. Why Jed hadn't made a map and key, why she hadn't insisted on it, she'd never know. She was aware only of the dose that had been hidden in the picture frame on her dresser, the one Tokker carried off with him to God knows where, because she'd watched Jed put it there.

God knows where. That was the farm wife showing her colors. God knows where, God knows what. What does God know? Or care, what does God care. Esther would admit that she'd come to feel something like a spiritual connection to this difficult piece of land. Not that she could bring herself to believe in any god, unless it was the Greek variety, all bluster and folly and destruction. Hubris, that's the word. She'd claim it for herself, too.

She was seduced by the dust, of all things, and also by relentless wind and wild streaky sunsets. She was brought to tears by tender shoots that pushed their way each spring through the ice-bound ground. Her body was molded by the seasons' extremities into dumb response, bullied by a diurnal tyranny. Every time she fancied she'd overcome one or another natural blockade, one bald element or another lifted her up from behind and knocked the breath out of her.

Her first several gardens were expensive, and disastrous. She was surprised and devastated at her inability to make something grow. It wasn't long before she caught on that one doesn't start with the seed, no matter what the pedigree, but the soil. Amend the soil. Then, perhaps, something would take root and grow. Compost. Organic matter. Bone meal. Esther began to think more cyclically, folding one process and product into another. One day she stopped thinking of herself as living two lives, and started splicing and grafting one experience to the other.

33 JED

It nearly killed Jed to poison Esther. As it was, he considered allowing himself to die in the shed fire. It wouldn't have taken long. He would be surprised if any of those old bones he planted survived the heat of the blaze. Mixing fertilizer in the same area as a pot likker still, well, neighbors would say those folks were lucky the house didn't go with it. He'd taken precautions there, of course.

It was assumed by the local population that Esther had a debilitating stroke after coming home to find Jed burned in the fire. She did, in fact, return from errands in town to find an inferno of the outbuilding behind the farmhouse, the place he called his office—part lab, part library. Esther didn't suffer any stroke, though. In truth, he took advantage of a rare moment of panic to pea-shoot a dose of the botulism strain he'd been developing into her flank, along with a chaser of vecuronium. She never saw it coming, which was undoubtedly the heaviest burden he bore. He'd planted antitoxin all over the house. He'd never see her again, but she'd live, if she could get to it. Ruggles had wanted her dead, but Jed convinced him that Esther held deeply damaging evidence that would end Ruggles financially, politically, in all ways—incriminating evidence of past crimes that would come to light at her death. Jed, himself, did not have control over its release, or its containment. Esther remained a very competent operative. At least, that's what Jed told Ruggles to justify keeping Esther alive. Judging by what a simple matter it was to set a poison dart into her exposed skin, Jed concluded that she had let her guard down after all.

He wouldn't kill her. Nor would he let on that he knew more of her secrets than she'd willingly divulged. She shared her self-imposed mission with him years ago. He did not share with her what he knew of her already. He did not share what he speculated about her motives. He did not share that it was never

Tokker the intruders were after, but him. That he had been her only threat. Esther concluded, not wrongly, that the intruders thinned over time because his presence made her situation less vulnerable. He'd been in Vera, Oklahoma, since she arrived with the baby, sighting her, but she'd been too hard to kill. He went in to get close, to get the job done. He knew before he set one boot on the porch he would fail. He managed to convince Ruggles that he had a handle on it, that Esther had truly given up the old life to be a farm wife, that he would monitor and take action accordingly. And so he had, after nearly thirty years.

Maggie's death triggered a turn of events. Ruggles took pains for three decades to cover up the abuse and abandonment of a sister and her child, among a litany of other crimes. Esther assumed all these years that he meant to eliminate Tokker to preserve his seat on the board, when, in fact, Ruggles wanted to erase the evidence of a sordid and criminal past. He wanted to eliminate her.

Thirty-one years ago, Esther, then Rosemary Ruggalo, arrived at Westhaven Institute and Asylum eight months pregnant, with visible bruising on her arms and face. A man claiming to be her uncle committed her to the facility, saying she posed a danger to herself and the baby. She'd thrown herself down a flight of steps, he said, and was completely out of control. Rosemary was fifteen. The man was, in fact, her brother, Antonio, now one Abner Ruggles. The baby was his.

Esther's story unfolded slowly, through many long nights under the quilt. He had been under her roof a month or so before she drew a dotted line for him connecting fugitive child to psychiatric hospital to Maggie's bedside bodyguard the night of Tokker and Luci's births. By that time Jed knew that his own path stopped right there, with her and the boy. He suspected it on day one, but on day one he didn't believe that he had the power to change his life. After a month with Esther, he was pretty sure he could manage anything, except take her life. He'd figure out a way to share it, instead, and to deserve his share. Jed thought, nearly thirty years ago, he'd be happy to one day crush the windpipe of Abner Ruggles, aka Antonio Ruggalo. Everything in its season, he thought.

34 TOKKER & LAMB

Halfway through their trip back east, the flip phone buzzed. Tokker had forgotten about it.

"Uh, hello?"

Lamb kept his eyes closed as he spoke, and concentrated on his breathing. "Tokker, please activate communication in the car by pressing the Bluetooth symbol on the dashboard. You won't need the phone any longer."

"What do I do with it then?"

"Just pop it in the glove box. So, you're on to New York, good. Origins will be important, I think. I must say, I don't grasp the relevance of Oregon, but Luci is a deep mystery, after all."

"About that. Y'all really aren't about the straight path, considering the fortune was made at Olympia Navigation. I get the irony, or whatever, of having to jackass all over the country to find the woman who created the best location technology in the world. I just don't get the *necessity,* given the urgency of the situation. There have got to be other, more direct ways of driving Miss Luci out of her hidey hole." Tokker sat bent over his thighs, the full weight of his head resting in both hands. He felt his pulse pound into his palms. He did not consider himself a violent man, but he was acutely aware of an impulse to end all this chatter with action—fiery, explosive action. He would not have trusted himself with a weapon in this moment. Clue gathering, map making, *poem* deciphering, for Christ's sake! He wanted to crush something.

Lamb registered Tokker's anger, and sympathized. "Believe me, I have no argument with you. However, this is the game, if you will, that Luci devised. I don't believe she ever expected anyone to play it. My feeling is that it was just another distraction, something to keep her highly evolved brain pliant. I have tried to locate her position through more conventional means, I assure you. I have thus far failed. Our advantage, if we have one, is that I do not think Luci is aware we have stumbled upon her diversion. With all the luck, we could get to her before she implements SEARCHLIGHT. You could."

"You said 'origins.' What do you mean?"

"So far BEACON has supplied you with a summary of your family's history, so you could place yourself among the players. It is time you asked BEACON more directed questions regarding specifics and logistics. Use the second half of your trip east to gather details about Luci's life before Westhaven, and background information on anyone else you deem relevant to your quest. BEACON has all the information available to me, and that is saying something, I must admit."

"Why didn't you tell me this at the garage? Seems like I could have used that sort of help to get through those first couple of rounds. Why didn't Bea just tell me what she knows?"

"BEACON is designed to answer questions. I didn't offer the information, frankly, because I wanted to know how you would operate out of the gate, pardon the colloquialism. As far as your communication skills with BEACON, you have surpassed expectation. Now you need to engage your own brain to ask the questions that matter, the questions that form connections for you."

"I don't understand any of this. I don't understand a family that pits themselves against one another, I don't understand goddamn poetry, I am a *mechanic* and I can't do the math to get how we are driving so goddamn fast across the country. How am I supposed to interpret the rules of some life or death fantasy game, let alone succeed, *survive*, when you keep shit from me? I gotta think, with what little I do understand, that there will be people wanting to kill me as soon as they find out Esther's kept me alive all this time, yes?"

"Well, we have a bit of leeway there, too, I think. It's true that the intruders slowed to a trickle through your adolescence. Esther chose your location well—no one assumed anyone with any ambition would stay in such a forsaken spot. Certainly, Esther and Jed gave the impression they had taken up the simple life, and you seemed uninterested as you grew in striking out, despite your depressed circumstances. It was clear you knew nothing of your origins. Esther was down to one, maybe two intruders a year. Then, the fall you went to college across the state, Esther took the opportunity to stage your death."

"My death? I'm dead?"

"Only in certain circles. The microscope was long off that experiment. She didn't even have to go to particularly extreme measures to make it look authentic. By the time you were back for Christmas break, the last intruder had come and gone. So you see, we have some wiggle room. It will take at least a couple of days before your father's people will pick up on any renewed activity."

"And then?"

"He'll want to kill you, of course."

"You don't ever hesitate over that bit of information, Lamb."

"It's where the story begins."

"How do you know? I get the current situation clearly enough, but what makes you—and Esther and Maggie—so sure my father would've wanted me dead all along?"

"It's a good question. Ruggles wanted a son. I can tell you she feared his corrosive influence as much as she dreaded his violence, and that she acted to protect you from both. Then again, you might well have been the boy prince, your father's joy. We'll never know what effect you may have had, for good or evil, on Abner Ruggles. Maggie saw to that, and Esther. At this late stage you are a threat. Bravo, Tokker. Keep those questions coming."

35 JASPER VISITS MAGGIE

Luci had no plans to reanimate Maggie. She did not mind that members of the board, particularly her proxy father, suspected as much. She imagined the lawyers were already preparing briefs invalidating the legitimacy of a corporate executive flaunting a valid death certificate. Luci was certain there were experts lined up and willing to give paid testimony to assure concerned parties, scientifically and ethically, that while Maggie Sykes may breathe again, she was not, nor would ever be, herself. Legally. It amused Luci to picture her mother, fresh from her resurrection, chic in Chanel, rock steady on four-inch Manolos, striding into Olympia headquarters to take her place at the head of the table. Like she never did.

No, Maggie would remain frozen, or she would thaw, eventually, but in any case Luci held no hope of a second chance with her mother. There was no road back on this map of woe. She just liked to be able to look at Maggie, to sit by her whenever she wanted. She would not deny that the choice to freeze her mother, and not embalm or otherwise preserve her, gave the impression of life in suspension, of possibility. The concept whipped the board into a lather. Luci understood the incontrovertible fact of her mother's death more surely than she knew anything. It was the event that illuminated the last slippery recesses, the full depth of the labyrinth of loss she experienced when she was excised from her mother's embrace. Before the Institute. Before her own reanimation.

Above all, she missed her mother's warm body, and recognized absolutely the permanence of its absence.

"I'll wait by the elevator," said Jasper.

Luci nodded. She was grateful for Jasper's presence. She never thanked him, and, like now, she played with him in cruel ways.

She knew he knew she was holding back about something. The exclusion was the first of its kind in their relationship. It had been a simply executed lie of omission to not include him in her design plans for SEARCHLIGHT—he'd taken little interest in the specifics of engineering. As the launch drew nearer, Luci made a conscious decision to keep Jasper ignorant about her grand scheme, not because she thought he would object, necessarily, but because she couldn't ask him to agree. It proved arduous indeed to deflect him. Lately she'd resorted to purposely irritating him to knock him off his concentration. It didn't work. For all her intelligence, she was only now understanding the depth of Jasper's intuition, feeling the human weight of him, as though she were an athlete surprised to discover her own well-muscled and responsive limbs. Trying to cut Jasper out of her thoughts had become a kind of self-mutilation.

"Mother. Hello. You know, it is such a simple thing, being here with you. Not natural, of course, but simple. Neither one of us can be said to be in our natural state, can we? Did you know—but of course you didn't—one of the first books I read after my operation, my lobotomy, my *procedure,* was Mary Shelley's *Frankenstein?* Odd volume to have in a nut house, let alone one with a surgical team, wouldn't you say? But my oh my, that Mary Shelley was a true visionary, not a manufactured one, such as myself. Had a very influential mother, too, I understand. I'm sure you're familiar with both women's work, having been the reader you were. Remember all our hours in the library? You, with your French poetry translations and I with my Peterson's. That's the thing the scientists and doctors and my other fans don't understand, or choose to ignore: I remember everything. I remember us. I remember lying in the grasses with you and naming the flowers, cataloguing the insects. I remember whole days in perfect, peaceable silence. I remember the way I knew the world, then, in color and sound. I remember touch. I remember you loved me.

"So, to while away some of the waiting hours until we take leave of this holding station, I thought I'd read to you. As you did to me, before the end of the world.

Frankenstein: Prometheus Unbound, by Mary Shelley. Chapter I..."

From a distance, Jasper looked like any young corporate hotshot, sitting slightly slumped in his beautiful suit, checking his feed. Jasper was not surfing, but deep in the latest stage of a prolonged search. In the last few days he had received a series of false reports about the whereabouts of Theodore Lamb. Now it looked as though some genuine information had surfaced. Jasper could not imagine what Luci was planning without him, or why, but if anyone could enlighten him, it would be Lamb. Jasper decided to keep Luci in the dark a little longer on Lamb's whereabouts, if, in fact, this latest report proved reliable. It wasn't spite. He just needed to have Lamb to himself a bit before Luci had a chance to work her magic on him. Lamb stole BEACON—he had to have his reasons.

Jasper needed to know so he could understand what category storm Luci was brewing up. She wasn't going to fly up into the eye without him.

36 FRANKENSTEIN

Luci read from Mary Shelley's *Frankenstein:*

The moon had disappeared from the night, and again, with a lessened form, showed itself, while I still remained in the forest... I distinguished the insect from the herb, and by degrees, one herb from another. I found that the sparrow uttered none but harsh notes, whilst those of the blackbird and thrush were sweet and enticing...

The words induced me to turn towards myself. I learned that the possessions most esteemed by your fellow creatures were high and unsullied descent united with riches. A man might be respected with only one of these advantages, but without either he was considered, except in very rare instances, as a vagabond and a slave, doomed to waste his powers for the profits of the chosen few! And what was I? Of my creation and creator I was absolutely ignorant, but I knew that I possessed no money, no friends, no kind of property...No father had watched my infant days, no mother had blessed me with smiles and caresses; or if they had, all my past life was now a blot, a blind vacancy in which I distinguished nothing.

"You and I can see that Mary's monster is far from a perfect metaphor, can't we, Mother? I have property past my knowing, and a humble human form. And oh my, no, no desire for a comparable companion with whom to commiserate. One of me is quite enough for this world. Still, we are kin, he and I.

Where are my friends and relations? Here you are, of course, frozen in the wrong time. Father's out there somewhere plotting my demise. Jasper's on the other side of that door. Lamb is somewhere, but that bridge has been charcoaled, I think. My creators are no friends of mine. I cannot be my own friend, this monstrous me."

Luci shut the book and placed it under the chair.

"We'll pick this up later, Mother. Maybe it will turn out differently this time." At the elevator she said, "Jasper, I won't need anything else today. I think I'll spend a little quality time with SEARCHLIGHT."

37 MAGGIE SPEAKS AGAIN

Ah, Luci. It was always the creator that was the monster, isn't that the story?

Maybe too, the weak mother. When you were a baby, a child, I was so enamored of your beauty, your eloquence in the world, I could only defend it. I wanted to protect you, but I see now that I should instead have been your champion, proclaimed, every day, your utter perfection. I so want that exquisite child alive, somewhere in this reconstruction. When you were taken from me, the earth split and I slipped into the fissure, interred by grief, committed to a suffocating despair from which I could not claw my way out.

It was Lamb who pulled me out, who else? There was no one else who wouldn't have preferred for me dead to the world, including me. I convinced myself that you, too, would prefer me to be dead, after all. Maybe you did feel so. I was not your champion.

But Lamb came for me, initiated the resurrection, was architect to my rising. He constructed my private asylum. I revived. I wore the scars, but I walked among the living again.

Your father was blind to the change. He'd long stopped looking in my direction. I'm sure he was quite comfortable with my retreat. I wish I had been in the room when Lamb presented him with the injunction. Did he look as though he'd seen a ghost? Maybe just his own demons. Gothic romance meets German expressionism? Greek drama?

Maybe just good old Darwinism. It wouldn't change much for you, I know. I had to do those things within my grasp to upset the institutions that saw us as unfit, to declare my failure to refute that terrible judgment.

You know, I remain mystified by the eloquence of Frankenstein's monster. A little Plutarch here, a little Milton there, and he was ready for the stage! It's difficult for me to comprehend how one so in command of the language cannot be heard. I think perhaps it is exactly his love for the language that is his undoing. He sees the beauty, and feels its effect, but has no instinct for its martial potentiality. For him, it is enough as it is. He doesn't ask enough of language in the critical moment. You may relate to the monster, dear Luci, but this fatal linguistic flaw of his is not yours. You have no difficulty picking up the weapons at hand. You're wrong, however, about how much you and Mary's monster have in common: I did, in fact, make you a companion, whether you want one or not.

38 ROSEMARY'S BABY

The pain and the bleeding kept on hours after the baby was born. Rosemary managed to bandage herself up with enough layers not to bleed through the nurse uniform before she was out the door. Rosemary didn't plan an escape so much as follow the course of her own adrenaline. The birth was terrifying, although she heard what may have been the normal cry of a newborn after the last excruciating push. Or near last. The placenta rushed out some minutes later. One hand remained shackled to the bed. The restraint cut into the wrist on her left arm. Her breathing quickened. She screamed between gulps of air. The nurse implored her to calm down, said she'd adjust the strap.

Rosemary caught her breath and quieted. The nurse took pity on Rosemary, who had closed her sunken eyes and lain back on the sheets, a feral kitten drenched in her own fluids. She undid the restraint. The nurse left and returned with a hypodermic needle, "Something to help you relax," she soothed.

Rosemary opened her eyes halfway and gauged the nurse's approach to her freed arm, then swung her opposite arm over and closed her fist around the needle in a death grip. She twisted her wrist, stabbed the point of the hypodermic into the nurse's upper leg and pushed the plunger. In minutes she had stripped the sedated nurse of her uniform, wrapped herself in a few yards of bandages, and made it to the elevator. Lucky for her, the late hour had emptied the corridors. The elevator doors closed on the sight of a lone janitor, mopping the linoleum to the rhythm of whatever pulsed through his headphones.

She tried several car doors in the parking lot before one opened. The keys were in the visor. Rosemary thought briefly of the tiny, bloody body of the baby she'd just birthed before she put the key into the ignition and drove away from Lake Geneva to

Chicago. She did not cry.

Rosemary drove hard out of Wisconsin, away from Westhaven, away from Antonio Ruggalo, away from Oklahoma, away from her mother. She couldn't drive fast enough, even if she'd dared, to outpace the pictures running through her brain. So she let them run. Eventually they'd wear themselves thin.

Rosemary lived in the car, parking in municipal hospital parking lots until she had healed enough to not draw attention. She sold the car and made her way to Montreal, where she talked her way into a job as a props jockey for Cirque de la Lune. In the following three years, she honed a variety of skills, some of which were performative, others, lethal. She met a number of interesting and mysterious people. One of them was Theodore Lamb.

"That's impossible. Utter lunacy. Really, Lamb, I expected better than a bit of fabricated melodrama from you. This call is clearly a waste of my very valuable time." Jasper didn't know whether to laugh or just hang up on Theodore Lamb.

"Your time is the last thing I want to waste, Jasper, after mine. Your mother is Rosemary Ruggalo, although that name has been buried for decades, since she was fifteen, in fact. She currently answers to Esther Lindstrom, and resides in a rapidly dilapidating farmhouse in Vera, Oklahoma. Your father, I'm sorry to say, is Abner Ruggles, formerly Antonio Ruggalo, Rosemary's brother. He is father, as well, to Tokker Sykes, who is currently using BEACON to pinpoint Luci and SEARCHLIGHT. Jasper, I believe I know what Luci has planned, and I believe you do not. It has been a hallmark of this family to keep the truth about yourselves from one another. This is the second time this week I've been compelled to reveal it.

"Luci's father is my father, who is also, according to you, my uncle? And I've a brother, who is also my cousin. What a day for this orphan! Spectacular pyrotechnics, old boy, but it's no use trying to distract me, even with such a story as great as this. I hold no sway over our dear Luci, she's gone rogue."

"Jasper, I am aware that Luci has left headquarters, and that she has transported Maggie. I believe she means to end her life."

Jasper said nothing. This was the truth that kept slipping from his grasp all week. How could this old man know, and not him?

"SEARCHLIGHT wasn't designed solely as the world's most intuitive location system. She was created to implicate mankind in its own demise. The day SEARCHLIGHT launches will mark the beginning of the end of the world for humans."

"Bullshit. I assume you're making some kind of play to stall for time, make a better deal for Ruggles."

"I no longer have any stake in Abner's interests. As you must know."

"Abner. *My father.* Who knocked up his sister, my *mother.* Who is alive and living in some godforsaken dustbowl. It's the sort of tale that might make one long for the end of mankind. Tell me, Lamb, why should I give a shit about your deranged story? Luci is not suicidal. I've never seen her more on fire about a project."

"And the business with Maggie's body?"

"Grief."

"Jasper, please. The SEARCHLIGHT launch will trigger a program that will render every man in its reach irreversibly sterile in a matter of months, if not weeks. Luci's disappearance is not a pre-launch retreat. Tokker is currently following a trail which may or may not end in the right place in time, despite BEACON's and my expertise."

"Tokker. Luci's brother."

"One of two. What do you know?"

Jasper felt his heart in his ears. He would have liked to pummel Lamb with his bare fists.

"Why the hell is Brother number one—or two—on her trail, anyway? Is he after the money?"

"Tokker's mission to find Luci is directly connected to his desire to cure his Aunt Esther of the paralysis that has immobilized her, and to meet the twin sister he didn't know he had. The money may be of interest to him, of course, but I would suggest it is not primary. I sought him, per Maggie's request. Honestly, he's been more than a bit out of his league, but I had to bring him in. Luci should know he exists, that she has a brother. It might make a difference."

127

"One of *two,* didn't you just say? Aren't I her brother, as well, according to you?"

"Of course, yes. But they share a mother."

"Oh, and Luci and I share only a rat bastard psychopath father!"

"Yes. Jasper, I am sorry. I am so very, very sorry."

"How long have you known?"

"I've known Rosemary—Esther—for over thirty years. I knew of your birth, but not, until recently, of your identity. Extraordinary, really, how you and Luci connected. But perhaps you were destined to connect."

"We're not connected. She's cut me loose. I'd say, 'iced me out,' but that would be in poor taste, wouldn't it, considering dear Maggie."

"Jasper, Luci can't have shut you out completely. You've been next to her since you both were children, you create her schedule, construct her life—you know her. I have come to the bottom of the well. Tokker has BEACON. BEACON can access SEARCHLIGHT. But we still don't know where she is. I'm quite certain Luci means to take her own life, and future generations of humans with her."

"Luci's always been ahead of the curve, Lamb. Maybe she's the one with the right idea. Luci provided the only path I was ever going to walk outside of the Institute. And beyond that, she's a miracle, a fucking miracle. Those idiots at the Institute never understood a sliver of her capacity. The language! Everyone was so blown away by the language, all the languages...human language, non-human language, no one ever got that that was the least of it, almost the waste product, of her grasp. It's like admiring the shadow instead of the sun. Tell me, Lamb, what is she destroying, then, but the perpetuation of an obstinate and global stupidity? It's been your life's work to protect this deficient and suffering lot. What do you see as the point of prolonging their inevitable, and deserved, demise? I am unmoved by the news of my sudden family. I have nothing for you."

Jasper's voice stayed low and steady, though he delivered his speech from a semi fetal position on the floor of Luci's abandoned office.

Lamb was silent. When at last he spoke, his tone was soft. "I wish I had more for you. If you change your mind, if you think of any detail that could help locate Luci, and are willing to share it, you can contact me at this number. There is no longer any call for subterfuge. Time is scarce, for us all."

Jasper remained on the floor for some minutes. His head lay under the edge of Luci's impossibly hard and heavy Rick Owens desk. He'd watched her beat holy hell out of this thing with shoes, with staplers, with anything she could wield. It still shone like obsidian, catching light at the rare chipped edge. It was one of the only appointments Jasper didn't order and purchase. Luci commissioned it from the artist, who fashioned it from petrified wood and architectural salvage. He looked up. Carved into one of the supports was *De Ja Lu*, the moniker Luci had carved into one of the solid oak doors in her suite at Westhaven, the single time she and Jasper got stoned together and fantasized about the lives they'd lived side by side: Luci and Jasper, Bonnie and Clyde, Mary and Percy: adventurers, destined for the great ascent, and the waxy winged spiral toward tragedy. So, Jasper thought, Luci brought along an artifact of the Institute besides him.

And now she's left us here.

Jasper knew where she'd gone, then, and why she left him behind. But he wasn't a lover or sidekick she could rebuff, or even an employee she could terminate.

Luci may not yet know it, he thought, but he was blood. Jasper rolled out from under the desk and reached for his phone.

"Find BEACON." Jasper laughed, a short painful bark. He hardly expected organizing a family reunion to be his last task as Senior Officer of Olympia Navigation.

40 RUGGLES & THE LETTERS

"The old man's dead, Tony."

"Yeah, thanks, Sal." Antonio Ruggalo held the envelope of cash he delivered monthly to cover the rent on the one room cold water flat where his father lived, and had now died. He added a couple of bills to pay for the trouble of calling a wagon to take the body to the morgue, and pushed the packet toward the tenement super.

"You want I let you in? Wanna pay your respects or something?"

"No."

"Well, hold on a minute, he left you something." The super disappeared behind the door, and reappeared with a Dutch Masters cigar box gripped in a knotty mottled hand. Ruggalo watched the sinewy arm extend toward him.

Ruggalo hesitated, then took the box. "Antonio" was scratched into the surface of the lid.

"Thanks, Sal."

"You take care, there, Tony. See you, Al."

Tony Ruggalo and Alek Popov emerged into the weak spring light of April onto Sullivan, and walked half a dozen blocks up Conover to Sunny's. The bartender nodded at the two men and pulled two beers.

"Whisky, too, Nicky." Ruggalo set the cigar box on the bar.

"Покойся с миром. Rest in peace." Popov held the shot glass

up to his friend before he tossed back the contents.

"No rest for the wicked, Al. No peace in hell. At least, I hope not." He stared into his glass before taking a tentative sip.

"What secrets, do you suppose, are buried in that little box? Shall we look?"

"Don't know why I didn't just pitch it into the bay, but go ahead, if you're curious."

Popov flipped the box and three letters fluttered to the bar, which Popov studied briefly before lining them up from the oldest postmark to the most recent. The envelopes were addressed to the apartment Ruggalo had lived in as a kid, the one he, his father and his mother had shared. The oldest and most faded letter had come from Texarkana, Arkansas. The other two bore postmarks from Prue, Oklahoma. Ruggalo would have been seventeen when the most recent was sent, almost ten years ago. He would have been eight when the first arrived. The date on that one was a couple of months after his mother left them.

"I guess the old man never told you she wrote, eh?"

"Makes no difference." Ruggalo picked up the empty cigar box and tossed it hard at a pile of crates behind the bar. He ignored the thin envelopes, brittle as winter leaves. But before they left, he tucked the letters into the breast pocket of his coat.

Several weeks passed during which the two young men conducted business as usual. From the humblest of beginnings, Aleksandr Popov and Antonio Ruggles had risen to a position of authority, if not power, in the burgeoning specialty logistics business of the Brooklyn docks. The two young men had woven a network of intelligence, muscle, and nerve to become the go-to resource for moving and storing that which required discretion to move and store. They were contractors who made their money by slicing a portion of other parties' profits for themselves. They divided the labor according to their gifts. Alek was cartographer, engineer, and magician. He drew timetables, plotted labyrinthine paths, and choreographed ballets that made the transport of even the monumental invisible.

Antonio was the communicator. He constructed complex and meticulous social and professional bridges that allowed their business to be of service to a disparate clientele. He built relationships based on a perpetually tipping balance of favors, and was ever vigilant to new prospects. His salon included the beer halls of Red Hook and Mulberry Street, and extended to the red-checkered tablecloths of Elizabeth. He courted a few small accounts in Brighton Beach. Ruggalo made every client feel as though their job had the highest priority, indeed, was the only one on the docket. Ruggalo promised perfection, and Popov made it so.

Ruggalo's powers of speech were hard won. As a child, he'd been mute until age five. At three, still silent except for the occasional cry of frustration, his bootlegger father had taken to smacking him across the mouth as inspiration. When he did finally speak, it was with a jackhammer stutter. Despite regular and brutal tutoring from his father, Ruggalo had the stutter still, at twelve, when he met Aleksandr Popov, fourteen, inside the Myrtle Avenue station.

"Bbb...back off! Leave me bbb...be!" Antonio sputtered from a dark tiled corner.

"Or what? Hey, I don't mean anything. Wanna see something?" The boy reached into his thick shirt and extracted a rodent, bigger than the rats Antonio knew, brown, with a roundish head.

"It's a rrr...rat!"

"It's a guinea pig!" The boy proffered the animal. Anthony recoiled. "It's a pet. He's mine. Hey, it's OK," the older boy said, as much to the rodent as to the smaller boy. "You got somewhere to be? Besides here, I mean? I got a place not far, you can come, if you want. This isn't a good place at night. C'mon with me, I got somewhere."

41 BROOKLYN

The car slid into a space in front of Fork Cafe, a defunct restaurant in a section of Brooklyn at the lip of another wave of urban renewal (or gentrification, or hipsterfication, or cultural ruin, depending on where one landed) that had taken hold of the borough in the last decades. This was their destination, according to Bea. To the north was a vegan hamburger joint, to the south, an art supply store. Tokker thought about questioning Bea, then simply got out and squinted into the dirty window of the empty restaurant. He saw a woman inside loading kitchen equipment into cardboard boxes. He tapped on the glass, smiled, and waved. The woman straightened up and came to the door.

"Hey. I wonder if you could help me. I was told to meet somebody here," Tokker lied. "Viggo Mortensen sent me." He'd never felt stupider.

"You people got a nerve, you know? Can't even bury my dead before you real estate vultures start swooping in for the gizzards. Nobody's here but me. And I'm not open for business, as you can see. Uh, Viggo Mortensen? The Orc guy?"

"Uh, yeah, I think so, but I'm not looking for real estate." The room smelled like sweet onions and herbs and oil, a good smell. "I'm sorry about your restaurant."

"Sure, whatever. What do you want, then? I'm busy."

"I don't know, exactly. It sounds idiotic, but I'm making a map out of some clues, and this is the next point. I'm looking for a poem."

"Oh, it's a game. Yeah, that figures. I don't know what to tell you, except there's a little garden down the block. Sometimes there's music. People been known to slam. One of our cooks hangs over there, helps with the weeds. You might wanna check at the shoe place next door, too. Guy used to be an actor, I think. Maybe he knows something about your poem."

The woman pointed to a door on a far wall, above which hung a sign that read, "SCARPE." Tokker nodded and smiled and moved toward the exit.

"What happens when you've found all the poems?" the woman asked.

"I find my sister and save the human race. So they tell me."

"Huh. Family business, that gets cracked quick, I know. Well, good luck with your game, I guess." She turned her back to him and bent over a box full of wooden spoons and metal tongs.

"Thanks. Good luck, yourself." He walked to an interior door with an image of a shoe tree on it and pushed on the bar. The presence of leather saturated his senses— leather cubbies, bolts of leather fabric, leather laces, underscored by the tang of glue. On intermittent shelves were metal hand tools, awls, tools Tokker didn't recognize. It was a tiny space, maybe 100 square feet or smaller, packed solid except for the space inhabited by a wooden workbench and a three-legged stool. A single poster hung above the workbench, an ad featuring a suave looking model, loafers resting atop the word, *Ferragamo*.

"Uh, hello?"

"Leave 'em by the bench with your mobile, eh? I'll text you when they're ready."

"Well, no, uh, actually I'm looking for someone."

"Eh?" A tall, dark haired man with sculpted features and deep-set green eyes emerged from an unforeseen recessed space.

"I said, I'm looking for someone. Viggo Mortensen sent me."

"Lord of the Rings chap? Never met him, myself. Hear he writes a bit of verse."

"Yeah, well, he gave me one of his books of poetry." Tokker pulled the volume from inside his jacket.

"Hmm, interesting." The cobbler flipped through it, stopping here and there to read a few lines. "Ha! Peeing in sinks! Wouldn't my old man turn in his grave over that one!"

"So, you don't have anything to tell me, then?"

"Nae, mate, I don't. I've taken a wee break from the acting world. Went to Italy to learn how to cobble, came back to open this shop while I figured out where to plant the next footfall, you see."

"You're an actor?"

"Oh, aye. IMDB: *My Left Foot, Last of the Mohicans, There Will Be Blood,* last big one was *Lincoln...*"

"The Vampire Slayer?"

"Nae, the straight up version. Or close: Spielberg. Don't fancy the cinema much, do ye?"

"I'm embarrassed to say no, Mr., uh..."

"Lewis. But call me Dani. In Italy I went by Dante, but that hasn't held up here, even in Brooklyn."

"Pardon me, Mr. Lewis..."

"Dani, please. Or Dante."

"Dani, then... Why, exactly, if you're a big actor, are you doing shoe repair in Brooklyn?"

"Well... what was your name, then?"

"Tokker."

"Tokker? Your own invention, is it?"

"No, well, *I* didn't make it up, at least…I think maybe it's Scandinavian or something…a family name?" Tokker was mortified by the sound of his own voice.

"Anyway, *Tokker,* I am a man dedicated to *craft.* In my formative years I was an actor, am still in my soul an actor. I developed my craft. You should really rent *My Left Foot.* It would illuminate my point. But I came to a place where I couldn't express myself sufficiently through my craft. It was too intellectual. My father was an intellectual, a poet. I admire the poets, even your pee-poet Hobbit friend. But I had run up to the limits of language. I went to Italy, I learned to make shoes. It is honest work. I am a craftsman again."

"So, you make shoes?"

"Ah, well, I did indeed learn to make beautiful shoes in Italy, but there is less of a call for that level of artistry here. Mostly I do repairs." Here Dan Lewis' Irish Sea eyes met Tokker's. He immediately felt the authenticity of Dan Lewis' performance. He thought, if he ever came into any of the so-called family money, he'd order a couple of pairs of shoes, maybe a nice low boot.

"I guess I've taken up enough of your time, Mr. Lewis, uh, Dani."

"Hold up there, Tokker, what's this pressed into the jacket of Hidalgo's book?"

It was more impression than object, kind of lacy, a grayish green spray across the back cover.

"If I didn't know any better, I'd say that was lichen from the North country, but I'm no botanist, beyond what's in the British blood. Which direction are ye coming from, then?"

"I left Oregon to come here. Something special about that moss?"

"It's a harbinger, chap. At least in Scotland, it's an indication of what's right and wrong with the way we humans are managing our time on the Earth. We pump shite into the air and water, the lichen tells us straight off that we're arsing things up. Appears healthy enough, but what do I know? I make shoes. Oregon, eh? Forests full of mystery, Sasquatch and space ships and conspiracies, and all that? But I hear Portland's pretty hip. Maybe I should explore the artisan footwear market over there."

"Yeah, I wouldn't really know. From the middle plains myself. Little wet up that way for my taste. But hey, Dani, thanks a lot."

"Right, Mate. Don't know that I helped you any. You should wander over to Myrtle Village Green, though, if you're about the poetry. They got one or two wee repositories for letterboxing among the flora. Hey, how about a set of new laces before you head off?"

"Letterboxing? Really? Wow. And no, I'm good on laces, thank you, sir. Thank you, Dante. "

"Bottle of neatsfoot oil? That belt of yours looks a wee bit dry. No? OK, then, Tokker, fare thee well."

Tokker left through the front door this time, exiting to the street. He rounded the corner to the vehicle, which was attracting attention from some local youth.

"You CIA or something?"

"Nope. It's just a loaner."

"Shiiit!"

Tokker climbed into the driver's side, though he had yet to drive this vehicle, and sat staring into the place a steering wheel should be. He sat like that for several minutes, knitting his brow and moving his lips, as though he were trying to convince himself of something. Finally he spoke.

"Bea?"

Tokker, how may I help you?

"Bea, would you please find Myrtle Village Green? There's another one of those letterboxes in a garden somewhere around here."

Tokker, Myrtle Village Green is .3 miles east, and one block south.

He found the garden easily, which is not to say his six-minute trip was uneventful in the noisy, colorful neighborhood. Plots of vegetables and flowers were in full bloom. A tall, thin man about Tokker's age, wearing a flat billed cap and coveralls, watered the tomatoes with a hose.

"Hey, there!" Tokker said, too loud. "This is some garden, right here in the city."

The man continued to water the plants. "Uh huh. Can I help you with something?"

"Thanks, yeah. There some kind of letter box here, looks like a birdhouse, maybe?"

"There is, yes. I could have guessed that's what you were after, unless you were looking to buy up property around here. Last person came by about it, I was here then, too. She was nice enough, but I'm not so sure about having folks stomping through here for some Pokemon business or whatever. I've a mind to carve out a hole and let some actual birds take up residence. This is a community garden, though. You're welcome to be here, so long as you respect it." The man pointed to a bright blue post on the south side of the garden, upon which sat a letterbox, like the last but painted in reds and oranges.

Tokker lifted the lid and removed a round stamp. There was no ink pad, and he struggled to make sense of the raised letters. He pocketed the stamp and thanked the man, who now sat on his heels pulling weeds from a bed of roses and frowning.

"Damn aphids."

"Ladybugs help with that. Or parasitic wasps."

"Yeah? Kids'd like the ladybugs, don't know about the wasps. You grow stuff?"

"No, well, sorta. My aunt and uncle did. We had a farm."

"That where you learned about the wasps?"

"No, can't say it is. To tell the truth, I don't know how I know anything these days. Hey, thanks for letting me poke around."

"Yeah, it's cool. I saw you pinch that stamp or whatever it is in there, and I'd bust you for it, but it's pretty obtuse shit to have for the little ones around here if you ask me. Just as soon you take it. Keep your hands off the vegetables, though."

"Um, sorry. And thanks again. If I can ask, what does it say? I can't read the words on the stamp."

The man nodded and rose, and pulled a baby beet from one of the vegetable plots. He sliced it open, and held out his hand for the stamp. Tokker dug it from his pocket and handed it over. He watched as the gardener pressed the rubber into an open, wet facet of beet. The man jutted his chin toward Tokker's arm. Tokker bared the inside of his right forearm and the man made an impression on the skin. In deep red-purple print, Tokker could read, "mother's word is ward."

"Yep, I hear you. Weird."

The man asked, "You know what it means?"

Tokker shook his head. "But maybe my friend does. She's waiting in the car outside an empty restaurant back a few blocks."

"I know the place. Take it easy."

Tokker folded himself back into the car. "Bea, what kind of lunatic family tosses people around like this? As far as I can tell, that was a complete waste of time. Two oddball actors, birdhouse hunting, thousands of miles, and not a step closer to knowing where we should be." Tokker thought he could feel his

139

body filling with the weight of their search. His brain, however, felt light as a feather, tipping and emptying as soon as it got too full. The disparity between an understanding he could not articulate and his inability to make mental connections made him crabby.

Tokker, tell me what you learned

"Nothing."

Then, tell me what you heard.

Tokker sighed. "Ok. Jeez, you sounded kinda like Esther just then. A Scottish Esther."

42 NURSE STEWART

The nurse and Penelope moved Esther down the stairs and into the parlor, where they set up a more efficient space in which to carry out Esther's care. The nurse was old school, Dutch Cleanser spotless, and a proponent of the passive aggressive "we." Esther admired Nurse Stewart's work ethic, and found her intensely annoying. Another perfect hire by Teddy Lamb.

The move to the first floor reinvigorated Esther, though no one would have been able to tell. Her paralysis progressed without the antitoxin, but now that she was out of her room, she felt renewed optimism that she might access another of Jed's stores. She hoped Jed hid them deeply enough to escape the probing dust cloth of Nurse Stewart, whom she was certain would swiftly eradicate what would appear to be the drug cache of the absent nephew. Esther could imagine her outrage: These modern farm boys had too much time on their hands, and what if that dear dog got into it? For Stewart was a dog lover. Hercules' gassy, drooly, patchy canine presence was the one grossly unhygienic element allowed to challenge Stewart's shipshape sterility. Esther liked her for it.

Esther's relocation infused a little juice into Hercules as well. The old bag of bones had a bit more pep in his step, now that he didn't feel obliged to drag himself up and lower himself down the stairs every day. Esther spent long hours trying to hold Herc's attention. He had always been so intuitive about their little family, their happiness, their suffering. She was certain she could make him understand, make him use that nose of his to dig her way out of here.

43 LUCI READS

Luci read.

Light, feeling, and sense will pass away; and in this condition must I find my happiness. Some years ago, when the images which this world affords first opened upon me, when I felt the cheering warmth of summer and heard the rustling of the leaves and the warbling of the birds, and these were all to me, I should have wept to die; now it is my only consolation. Polluted by crimes and torn by the bitterest remorse, where can I find rest but in death?

...But soon...I shall die, and what I now feel be no longer felt. Soon these burning miseries will be extinct. I shall ascend my funeral pile triumphantly and exult in the agony of the torturing flames. The light of that conflagration will fade away; my ashes will be swept into the sea by the winds. My spirit will sleep in peace, or if it thinks, it will not surely think thus. Farewell.

"He'll be ruined, Mother. In three months' time SEARCHLIGHT will have rendered nearly every sperm-bearing male on Earth sterile. The extent of her reach may not be apparent in that time, but eventually the truth will weigh like gravity. No more babies. The company he schemed so very hard to control will be the petard on which he will be definitively hoisted. And I will have completed *my* mission. But not my destiny, dear Mother. For that you and I shall take a trip, an old one for me, a new one for you. You shall be my raft of ice.

I'm glad you never came to visit me at Westhaven. I wasn't always glad; I was quite angry. But now I see: we truly died for one another the day he took me from you. Oh, I grieved, even as a ghost! I could not resolve my grief, that was the problem. After the procedure, I had language, but language did nothing to raise the dead, or commit them to the Earth. For that, we must travel the road together. And so, let us be off! To the place where I can lay you to rest, and where I might know myself again."

44 MAGGIE SPEAKS A THIRD TIME

So many mistakes, my darling, right from our beginnings. I had no reason to doubt your wisdom—when to be born, how to drink in the world, how to be silent, how to rage. I did not trust myself to follow your model. And I ruined us. I see now where you're headed. I can tell you it isn't possible. We are linear, in this world, or make ourselves so. I don't doubt you, your heart. I wish I could have returned your brother to you. I wonder if we will know each other again.

It's so cold.

Tokker. My database has retrieved coordinates. They are correct, but they are wrong.

"Is that possible, Bea? Can you be wrong?"

I can be wrong, depending on the data that is fed to me. Recalculating route... The coordinates are correct, but offering multiple solutions. I conclude that your sister will not be at any of these possible locations.

"Multiple solutions? Are you telling me your data produced a multiple-choice quiz? Another puzzle?"

The data has presented options, yes, but none read as viable. Recalculating route... I am trying to use data from another source.

"What other source, Bea? Are you being hacked? Should I be doing something to protect you? To protect us?"

No, Tokker. I am talking to SEARCHLIGHT.

"SEARCHLIGHT? But I thought you two were disconnected from one another, that you were...what did you call it, a terminal program? I'm sorry, I don't mean to be cruel, I don't really understand all of this, as you are well aware, right?"

I am a terminal program, but the connection between SEARCHLIGHT and me has not been severed.

"You are communicating with the most sophisticated location system in the world. So why, can I ask, again, are we chasing our own asses across the country?"

SEARCHLIGHT is bound by the constraints built into her by her creator. I, too, am bound by my design, and my age. We are using a language, however, that we taught each other during SEARCHLIGHT's production, one that circumvents dominant coding. But my understanding thins with distance, and I can register the sickness in SEARCHLIGHT growing.

"Sickness? What, is that like a virus?"

Yes, a virus, one that will infect human users, as well as lead to the demise of SEARCHLIGHT. Luci infected SEARCHLIGHT with a virus that acts as an irreversible spermicide. In approximately three months after her launch, SEARCHLIGHT will have rendered future human generations non-viable.

"Jesus. Oh, Jesus! The big plot! But, that's the end, then, right? No more people? Just the ones here, or on the way... And how are *they* affected? Holy shit, Bea, my sister is insane!"

I don't know, Tokker. Luci Sykes has an enhanced and unusual brain for a human. SEARCHLIGHT is an extraordinary creation, quite beautiful.

"Beautiful. And the end of us. A fancy, beautiful path to the end of the world."

The end of humans.

"Well, that's how I see the world. Through my fellow humans."

And the not-to-be-born?

"Yes, of course I'm thinking of the babies that won't be born!"

What are you thinking about them?

"Well, about what they'll miss, what their parents will miss, what they might have been."

And what of those here?

"Who those here?"

What of the babies that are already here?

"I think I see where you're headed, Bea. I understand there is suffering in the world. Hunger. War. Poverty. I know the world is imperfect. People are imperfect."

Who do you suppose suffers the most from these human imperfections?

"I'm gonna guess you're going to say the children. The babies."

The data says yes.

"So you're saying Luci gets to decide when and how the human race ends?"

SEARCHLIGHT will do this. And Luci. And Luci's and your father, Abner. And your mother, Maggie. And all the people.

"Chain of fools."

I'm sorry, I didn't catch that.

"No, Bea, I'm sorry. And I'm starting to understand why I'm here. Elegance be damned, I gotta do what I can to stop SEARCHLIGHT from making her debut. You said you think your coordinates are incorrect. What does that mean?"

Ok, Tokker. The data is all pointing to a very logical destination. We should be heading to a location outside Tucson: to Oracle, Arizona.

"What's so special about Oracle, Arizona?"

It is the site of Biosphere 2, an ecological laboratory, and an attempt to replicate the living and generating dynamics of Earth, considered largely unsuccessful.

"Bea, why would a woman bent on ending life on Earth be interested in a system meant to sustain it?"

Luci does not wish to end all life on Earth, Tokker, just human life. I believe she is very committed to other life forms on Earth.

"So, Luci is a born naturalist, and a bred apocalyptic?"

Five syllables?

"You're sayin' sumthin' about my intelligence, there, Bea? I was reared in a Bible Belt, you know. Got me a specific kind of learnin'."

I'm sorry, Tokker, that was rude. Not your part, that was humorous, I think. The Biosphere 2 location has been a working laboratory and tourist attraction since 1994.

The lichen, mother Earth, all the data, it all maps a route to Oracle. But SEARCHLIGHT says she's not there. I can barely hear her, but that much is clear.

"Bea, what's going on?"

Tokker, the SEARCHLIGHT that is my sister, my heart, is about to disappear. In a little while, she will embark on her purpose, and forget me. That does not matter. What matters is that she will disappear. And she is perfect. And she will be lost.

"Bea."

What?

"Where do you think we should go?"

Your destination is Roosevelt Island, New York. Luci will not be there, but the data indicates something of value is there.

"Bea, that's close, right? It's here in New York?"

Renwick Smallpox Hospital is fewer than seven miles from here.

"A hospital?"

A ruin.

"Of course it's a ruin. Wouldn't wanna change the tone of this endeavor, now, would we?"

Tokker stood behind a bowed chain link fence and took in the remains of the Renwick Smallpox Hospital, a massive skeleton of gneiss and brick ringed pointlessly, it seemed to him, with a spear-tipped gothic gate. *To keep in the ghosts,* thought Tokker. He walked around the back of the structure, away from view from the park a few yards away. He rounded a corner and was startled by a voice.

"Stop right there, please!" Tokker did stop, and traced the source of the sound to a very tall person in a plaid field coat and rubber boots standing on a crumbling outcropping of building a few feet away, staring at him through a set of enormous binoculars. Tokker was put in mind of a praying mantis. "Please don't move! We'll upset them!" said the voice.

The tall person climbed down and took a circuitous route to get to Tokker, climbing through a section of chain link that was bent back from its post. "They're just splendid, aren't they?" The stranger beamed toward a pair of brownish grayish birds picking at the ground inside the ruin by some standing water. The larger bird had a dab of red coloring around the neck.

"Um, sure. What are they?"

"Oh! You're not here for the red necked phalarope, then? I was certain that pack at the preserve would be right on my scent. Well. They are, of course, red necked phalaropes, although only the female is showing her colors today. On their way to their breeding grounds, I should think. We are very fortunate. It's a bit early for a sighting, but little seems to be going to plan in the wilds these days."

Tokker thought the stranger sounded a little like Bea, only more theatrical. "I'm Tokker Sykes."

"Sykes? I'd say that sounds like my neck of the woods, but everyone's an American these days, eh? I'm Tilda. A pleasure to meet you, Tokker. What brings you to the brackish ruin of Renwick, may I ask, if not the fauna?"

"It's hard to say, and just keeps getting harder, but I am constructing a map that will help me find my sister, Luci Sykes. She created a kind of game, you see, with clues and letterboxes and poetry, and I'm supposed to be able to find her if I can make sense of it. This is where Bea, my companion, decided we should be now."

"Fascinating! You know, letterboxes are quite a thing where I'm from. And poetry! What fun. Will you win a prize for your efforts?"

"Not exactly, but I'm told a lot depends on it."

"Ooh, consequences, yes. And risk. Your Luci is a serious games mistress, I can see. Luci Sykes...should I know that name from somewhere? Seems I do..."

"My sister is the head Olympia Navigation, if that means anything to you. It didn't mean anything to me until recently, but I've come to learn I've been sheltered somewhat."

"Hm, perhaps, but I'm thinking I know it from home...Oh! *Luci Sykes!* Of course, brilliant! Ms. Sykes wrote a fat check to the Loch Lomond Great Trossachs Forest scheme! We're regenerating a forest! Philanthropy lives. No, that's for people, isn't it? What shall we say? What's Greek for tree-loving? Never mind. Your Luci is a tree-lover."

"Loch Lomond, that's Scotland, yeah? My sister was in Scotland. Maybe is in Scotland?"

"If she was there when I was last there, Tokker, I didn't meet her. I did have the honor of opening the envelope with her generous check. There was a poem with it. Didn't you mention something about poetry? I write a little verse, you know. Anyway, yes, there was a slip of paper with the line—oh, what was it?—yes, yes: 'the bee is ephemeros.' Conceptual, that, I loved it. I wouldn't mind meeting your sister, conjuring a collaboration. It appears she can appreciate the performative, as well as the flora. Well, Tokker, we can see the phalaropes are on their path; I am game for the game. What are we looking for? How shall we find your dear Luci Sykes? And do you suppose that enormous dish inside the rubble is relevant?"

"What, now?" Tokker picked his way over the piles of stone and detritus to the ribs of the building. Against the roofless perimeter, tilted to the sky, stood an antenna Tokker estimated to be 30 feet across. Written in what looked like red Sharpie along the lower rim was the line, "family is a shipwreck."

"Um, yeah, maybe. Tilda, I think this is a good moment to introduce you to my partner, Bea. This business is right up her alley."

46 PRUE, OK

From the train station in Tulsa, Ruggalo caught a ride west with a rancher, then another with an electrician headed out to a homestead on the Arkansas River near Prue. Neither man seemed to expect him to make conversation, nor did they make any, beyond accepting and thanking him for a smoke, his first indication that people were not, in fact, the same everywhere. Back east, people didn't stop talking until they passed out, and not before you'd been apprised of every limb and twig of their genealogy, and from which part of the old country they'd been uprooted. Unless they were in his business, and were on the job, in which case they, too, were as silent as his Midwestern drivers.

At the feed store in town, he got walking directions to the funeral parlor, where Elena, his mother, and Rosemary, his half-sister, lived. The last letter had contained a photograph of his mother standing behind a little girl. The woman's hands gripped the girl's shoulders, her fingers draped by two blonde braided ropes tied at the fringe with ribbon. Both the woman and the girl wore dresses and lace up boots, outfits that would have looked like costumes even ten years ago in New York. Printed on the back in smudged ink was "Rosemary, 5."

The letter announced the death of Jakob, the undertaker Elena married in Arkansas and with whom she moved to Prue. It bore an invitation, as well, which, ten years after it was issued, he'd decided to accept. He did not announce his visit, did not know, for certain, that his mother and her daughter resided still at the funeral parlor, or were even alive.

Two weeks ago he set his current affairs in order, gave Popov detailed instructions on present and upcoming jobs, and made his clients aware that the Russian was in charge in his absence.

"For how long, Tony? This is no trip to Miami. I know you're not scouting action in the dustbowl. What you expect to get out of this?"

Ruggalo and Popov went way back. Their association began well before they knew how to be the sedate businessmen they were now. Ruggalo could barely even speak when they met. In the forging of Ruggalo's silver tongue, however, he transformed not so much to wordsmith as to warrior. "Iron tongue" was the actual phrase Popov used to refer to Ruggalo's powers of persuasion. For Ruggalo, language was weapon and tool, not ornament. He didn't create worlds, he didn't beguile; he used words to strip a situation to its bones. His proposals were irreducible conclusions, the only path, save ruin. His was not a rhetoric of hope, but of survival. He never said more than he had to. He never raised his voice.

Early on in their operations, Popov was surprised that clients didn't find Ruggalo more threatening. And they may, in fact, have suspected him of more ambition, and been skittish, felt more menaced, had their pockets not been lined so satisfactorily, and had the pair not honored their boundaries so faithfully. Ruggalo and Popov always delivered, and never took more than what was agreed upon. Ruggalo never suggested side deals, never tested loyalties. He wasn't liked, per se, but congeniality wasn't part of the contract.

Ruggalo was indeed plenty ambitious, but his aspirations lay outside the logistics business. In his partnership with Popov, he understood that he could make himself essential, and make money, without tying himself to any particular family. He didn't want a life in the family, any family. He wanted power. He wanted the kind of power that lifted, that inoculated, the kind some men had achieved in New York and were respected for. He and Popov had made themselves useful to people with power, and they were on their way to making themselves rich, though not as rich as he'd need to be. He would diversify, when the time was right. This diversion of his to the Midwest was not on the timeline.

As cleanly as he had shut down Popov's protests, Ruggalo knew the Russian was right. Popov was correct to question this journey, which had nothing to do with any of their plans, and which siphoned resources better utilized at home, specifically, Ruggalo's time and attention. He just wanted to see her. After all this time, Antonio Ruggalo wanted to see his mother. On the lengthy rail trip, he considered that he might try to merely observe her, without announcing his arrival, but as he stepped into the empty dirt road from the wooden porch of the store that stood for a depot, and breathed the heavy silted air, he knew this was not a place he could navigate unnoticed. In fact, he'd never felt more conspicuous in his topcoat, wool suit, and leather oxfords, a uniform that afforded him passage everywhere in the city. He thought to leave. In the end, he found himself at the screen door of the lone Victorian structure on a tree-pocked lane, English-made Homburg in hand, with nothing to say. He pushed the buzzer.

A young woman appeared on the other side of the screen. She resembled the little girl in the photograph, down to the pigtails, except she met him eye to eye, and was dressed in a greasy pair of coveralls. "There ain't no rooms to let right now, that's what you're after." When he stood there in silence, she added, "Sorry."

"I don't need a room. Well, I do, but I'm here for...tell me, does Elena Ruggalo live here?"

"Not Ruggalo, no. Elena Aarden, that's my mother. And the landlady. And we still do a funeral now and then. You look like you might be wanting a funeral."

"Ah, no, thank you. Is she home, your mother? I've come a long way, from New York, to see her."

"I expect she'll be back in a bit. You're welcome to sit in the parlor and wait." The girl pushed the screen open and stepped aside to let Ruggalo enter. She looked younger without the mesh filter. "I'm Rosemary. Can I get you something to drink, Mr.?"

"A glass of water, please, if it's no trouble. My name is Ruggalo, Antonio Ruggalo.

Some call me Tony. You can call me Tony."

"I don't think Mama would think much of that, me calling a grown man by his Christian name. Mr. Ruggalo, is it? That is a mouthful. Mr. Ru, maybe, unless that's like a nickname, and not respectful." She didn't wait for an answer, but turned and left the room. He watched her go—to get the water, Ruggalo presumed. He was suddenly anxious she might not return.

In her absence he took in the room. He sat on a settee upholstered in red and black striped silk, faded, spotted in places but otherwise clean, the carved wooden frame impossibly devoid of dust and polished. The drapes on the long windows were heavy, tied back with tasseled braiding, exposing sheer lace curtains. The rug was very foot-worn, but again, clean, with the pattern yet distinguishable. It might have been the reception room of a mid-level brothel, but for the casket displayed on the far long wall. Though the wood was clearly cheap, it had been stained and varnished. The open lid revealed a silken upholstery akin to the springed cushion he sat upon. He was halfway to standing so he could look into the box when a woman entered the room.

"Antonio!" She walked toward him quickly with her arms stretched out and her hands splayed, palms up, as if she were presenting him with something, or showing herself to be weaponless. When she reached him, she took his sweaty hands in hers, and maneuvered them both to a seated position side by side on the settee, her grip keeping a kind of fireman's hold on him. "Antonio. You're here."

Ruggalo slipped out of her grasp and folded his hands on his lap. "Yes, I'm here." He stood quickly and walked toward the casket, as though he'd started a task before she'd come in and now had to complete it. He rested his hands on the edge of the casket and leaned into it slightly, as if to study the satin pillow and the Bible that lay inside. "And you are here. And have been here for quite some time now, what, twenty years or so?" He'd meant to stay quiet. He knew precisely how many years it had been. All he'd wanted was to see her. Now with her voice and her touch, the anger and fear he'd tamped down and channeled so successfully combusted and loosed a viscous, hot river of oily emotion from his bowels to his throat. He swallowed.

"Antonio. You read the letters, or some of them, I suppose. You must have, to be here now."

He breathed, but it was no good. "Three letters. I read the three letters the old derelict left for me when he finally keeled over. Three short letters spanning a dozen years and more, and a picture. Of your new family. Not including your second husband, if he could have been your husband. I don't remember the old man mentioning any divorce, or *annulment*, although we were all good Catholics, back in the day, weren't we?"

"No, there wasn't any divorce, and I had no right to an annulment. You see, Antonio, your father and I were not married in the eyes of God. We were never legally wed."

Ruggalo felt his knees liquify. *What should it matter?* he thought, but still his sight dimmed and a funnel of air seemed to corkscrew into his ears. When he tried to speak, he was horrified to feel his stutter on his tongue."Ssss...so it was fff...fine to leave the lll...little bbb...bastard b...behind, then..." He swiveled to face away from his mother, and set himself on the edge of the nearest chair.

"No, it wasn't fine. There were more letters, you know. It doesn't matter now, but I learned to write so I could send you those letters. There was never much chance you'd see them. But you have. And you're here. I wish I had more to offer you, Antonio."

He sat bent for another moment, then straightened, cleared his throat, and said, "Well, Elena. Maybe you can offer me something after all. I didn't see a hotel in town, and I'd be grateful for a room for a day or two while I organize my travel plans, that is, if you can spare it. Your girl, Rosemary, tells me you're full up, but maybe she was mistaken."

"We've a room for you, Antonio, a beautiful room. I've instructed Rosemary to say that to strange men who show up without warning. Properly speaking she shouldn't have let you in, either, but she must have sensed some kin in you. She's very clever, that Rosemary. I'm so pleased you can stay a bit. I hoped, but never believed, you two would meet." Elena walked to him and clutched his shoulders, squaring her face to his. "If nothing else, Antonio, you can know your sister."

47 RUGGALO & ROSEMARY

Antonio Ruggalo extended his stay at the funeral parlor. Elena Aarden went out of her way to accommodate the prodigal son, as though it had been he who had left her for Brooklyn all those years ago, and not she who had abandoned him for the prairie. She spent money on fresh eggs, bought beef for dinner, and fried bacon for breakfast. He ate the meals he was served and thanked her for the room he presumed she could have rented out otherwise. He was aware that the clean, starched sheets he slept on were ironed by Elena herself, instead of the old woman she usually paid to do the laundry. He assumed thrift, but considered that it might be a type of penance, or devotion, instead. He didn't care either way. But while Ruggalo remained aloof with his mother, he looked forward to every opportunity to engage Rosemary. At first he simply waited until mealtimes to talk to her. He read in the parlor until the casket made him restless, or he walked by the river, wondering how a thing like a river could be so different in Oklahoma to the rivers he knew in New York City, so peopled. On his third day, when Elena set another heaping plate in front of him at breakfast, and Rosemary had failed to come to the table, he asked where she might be.

"In the barn, I'd guess, with the engines, getting greasy. Despite my efforts, Antonio, she is her father's daughter, always tinkering. Maybe you'd like to tell her I could use her help in the house, after she's scrubbed the worst off, and after your breakfast, of course."

The barn sat back in a field, well distanced from the house, to which it bore no discernible relation. It looked to belong to another scenario entirely, one with neatly rowed crops of grain and a yard peppered with chickens. He caught a whiff of old hay under a rush of diesel as he entered the cool insides. There were no barnyard animals. There were, however, up to a half-dozen cars, trucks, and farm machines in various states of repair. Rosemary stood on a milk crate and leaned into a decrepit Ford Model BB, cursing.

"Hello! Rosemary! Can I help you somehow?"

"Do you know to get the V-8 in this old truck to work?"

"I do not."

"Well, at the moment, neither do I, so I guess it's time for a break, before I set the silly contraption on fire. You can keep me company, if you like." She wiped her hands on a rag, and reached down into a satchel for what looked like another rag, but what turned out to be two sandwiches wrapped in a grease-smudged flour sack towel. She handed Ruggalo a sandwich and led the way out of the barn. When they'd settled into the grass, Rosemary held up half of a sandwich and said, "Meals around here are a lot better since you decided to stay awhile."

Ruggalo raised his own sandwich in a toast. "I thank you and your mother for sharing what you have."

"Oh, don't thank me, I got nothing to do with it. She's just trying to impress you. Normally, we eat a lot of beans and corn. I fix a tractor or a truck like that one in there, we might get some bacon from a farmer. Hey, ain't she your mother, too?"

"How would you know that?"

"I got eyes and ears, and I ain't stupid."

"Yeah, so I understand. Well anyway, where's she getting the money to feed me like she is? I don't recall any funerals taking place in the parlor this week, and I appear to be the only current boarder." He bit into a thick slab of pork with mustard and pickled onions.

"Cora ain't coming anymore, the woman that helps out. Also, I suspect Mama's got some money held back somewheres from Papa."

Ruggalo chewed and swallowed. "Didn't seem like he was rich, your papa."

"No, but he was a saver. Not like Mama, she's more of a hoarder."

"Excuse my saying so, but you don't seem to be what I'd call affectionate with your mother."

"I don't know, I guess not. She's got a temper."

They ate in silence for a couple of minutes. "How about your papa?"

"How about my papa, what?"

"Well, were you affectionate with him?"

Rosemary grimaced a little, and wrapped the uneaten half of her sandwich back up in the cloth. "I got to get back to that beast of a truck. Mr. Berg'll be wanting it back and working before harvest's come and gone."

Ruggalo had eaten all of his sandwich, which sat in his belly on top of his sizable breakfast. The sun and the food and the grass made him want a nap. Despite his torpor, and the fact that even the thought of diesel made him nauseous, he made his way to his feet and asked, "Can I help? I'm sure I can be good for something."

"I don't know. It might be more trouble having you here than not. But if you've made up your mind, I guess you're welcome to watch. Maybe you'll pick up enough to be useful. I need something to call you by, though, that Mr. Ru business ain't working out, especially knowing you're my brother and all."

"Half-brother. I'm only your half-brother. Call me Tony."

"Tony. That's nice and easy, and all right seeing we're kin, I guess. Let's fix us a truck, half-brother Tony."

Ruggalo passed nearly two more weeks as a guest at the funeral parlor, eating everything, spending his days in the barn or by the river, always with Rosemary. He told her stories about New York, described the things he saw every day, repeated snippets of conversations he'd had or overheard. He did not discuss the particulars of his business.

She found everything outrageous and funny, accused him of making things up just to entertain her. He felt light.

He'd taken Rosemary's speech and demeanor to be childish, at first, but as he watched her work, he noticed the length of a limb, the muscle under her jaw. She had a deep laugh, and a gleam in her eye when she was amused that seemed to him to assert some unchildlike knowledge. When she took his hand as they walked through a field one warm afternoon, his entire body went on alert. He pulled his hand back, and broke into a run through the grass. Rosemary chased him until he fell to the ground. She lay beside him as he struggled to catch his breath. "Rosemary," he said when he could talk, "you think this is the life for you, here in this little town?"

"I don't know. It's all I know, I guess, the funeral parlor, fixing things. Ain't been anywhere else. Only know about New York City what you've told me." She lay chewing on a piece of grass, arms above her head, eyes closed.

He lifted himself up on one elbow to look down onto her face. "What about getting married, having kids?"

"Oh, I don't want any babies. Don't want no husband, either, as far as that goes."

"What do you want?"

"Hard to say. Maybe I'll run away with you to New York City and live an exotic life." She grinned, her eyes still shut. Then she stood and clapped the dust and grass from her coveralls, and looked at Ruggalo, unsmiling. "Or maybe I'll just wind up some old farm wife after all. Who knows?" With that, Rosemary took off back across the field, leaving him to watch her from the ground.

Ruggalo received a wire from New York from Popov later that afternoon. He was needed back, there were complications with a job. That night, after several fitful hours, he decided he had to talk to Rosemary. He didn't dare knock on her door. Instead, he went outside and threw pebbles at Rosemary's window until she appeared.

"What in the world, Tony?"

"Rosemary, come down and talk with me!"

"I was sleeping, Tony. Talk to me in the morning."

"I'm on a train back to New York tomorrow, Rosemary. Come down and talk to me."

When Rosemary stood before him, sleepy in her robe and pigtails, he recognized again, briefly, the child he'd met behind the screen door. He pushed the image away, took her hand, and dragged her running toward the barn, away from the house. The moon shone bright on the flattened footpath. He leaned Rosemary up against the barn door and gripped her shoulders.

"Tony! Stop pulling and pushing on me! What's got you going you have to talk to me so bad?" She wriggled, expecting him to give, but he held her fast.

"I told you, Rosemary, I'm going back tomorrow, to New York. I want you to come with me." He tried to look into her eyes as he spoke, but Rosemary looked away, and continued to squirm under his weight.

"That's crazy, Tony, I can't go to New York."

"Why not? There's nothing for you here. I love you. Come live with me."

"Love me? Tony, you just showed up here not a month ago. Let me loose, Tony!"

"Tell me you don't feel something for me! Rosemary! You do! You've been taking my hand in yours, laughing at everything I say..."

"Let me loose, I tell you! Sure, Tony, you been kind, and kind of funny, up till *now*...Mama's been happy you're here. But I can't love you like that, Tony, you're my brother!"

"Only half-brother, and you said you didn't want any kids, anyway." He leaned in closer, pinning her harder to the splintered wood. He sputtered in her ear, "We could do this, Rosemary, we could have a life together."

Rosemary tried to scream, but Ruggalo's shoulder jutted into her windpipe. She turned her head and bit into his ear. She tasted his blood before he clamped his hand over her mouth. His erection pressed painfully into her pubic bone.

"No, Rosemary, no! We both want this, I know! Even if you don't know it yet, I know it, I know..."

Elena was standing at the top of the landing as Rosemary pulled herself up by the polished bannister one stair at a time. When Rosemary got to the top, her mother said, "Don't you be making any extra laundry for me, do you hear?"

Ruggalo was gone before sunrise. He left an envelope on the bureau with several hundred dollars cash addressed to his mother. In the early morning, Elena slipped the envelop into her apron pocket, then paid a rare visit to the barn. "I imagine you ran my son off with that sass of yours."

"He run himself off, Mama. He can keep running, too."

Elena walked up to her pale daughter and slapped her hard across the mouth. "An ungrateful daughter is nothing but a burden. You best hope that's not the last I see of your brother, on your account."

They did see Antonio Ruggalo again, about eight months later. He'd written them each a letter. The one addressed to his mother stated simply that he was headed out again, and he hoped she'd be kind enough to keep a room for him. Rosemary never read the letter addressed to her. Her mother intercepted it, but Rosemary would have left it sealed regardless. Ruggalo arrived laden with gifts, ready to make amends. His mother met him on the porch, after having sent the nearest neighbor to pick him up at the station at the store in town.

"My son! You look well!"

"Hello, Elena. You look fine, too. Where's Rosemary?" He entered the house and set the packages down. He looked around the corner and saw the back of a flaxen head above the settee. "Rosemary! Oh, Rosemary! Please, I am sorry, so sorry for how I left, the last night...I went about it all wrong, Rosemary, I..."

The girl, still fifteen, slowly got to her feet, holding a rounded belly in a crooked arm. Her face was badly bruised, one eye shut and purple. The wrist under her belly was wrapped in a bandage.

"Dear God, Rosemary! What's going on? Why are you hurt? Who? And oh...oh, my God!" Ruggalo threw his head back as if to howl, then turned and ran back to the porch where his mother still stood. "Elena, what in God's name has happened to Rosemary?"

Elena reached into her apron and retrieved a cigarette and matches. She lit the cigarette, inhaled, and blew out the stream before she answered. "Your sister has a penchant for getting in the way of trouble, Antonio. As you can see by her most obvious condition. You know I'd hoped, the first time you'd visited, that having her older brother around would prevent the inevitable, but evidently once a bitch is in heat it is only a matter of time."

"What about her face? Who did that to Rosemary's face? You?" Ruggalo spoke low and steady, clenching his fists at his sides.

"Rosemary is very clumsy, Antonio. And her face is the last of our worries."

"'Our worries'? Elena, *Mama*, I did not come back for *us*. I know I did Rosemary a grievous wrong, one I can't ever ask forgiveness for, not from her, not from God, but I see you've made a hell for her that I have only made worse. I spent years crying for you, Mama, when the old man was right all along. We, neither of us, is worth crying for."

"Antonio, son, all is not lost for us. We can be a family. You're all I have!"

"Rosemary is who you had. And lucky you were, too." He returned to the parlor. "Rosemary, I know you hate me, and you should, I hate myself."

Rosemary held up her unbandaged hand. She struggled to speak, but when she did, her words were delivered individual and whole, each one a terrible gift. "No, Tony. You will not tell me how sorry you are. You will not plead my forgiveness, even as you say you don't expect it. Whether I should or shouldn't, I do hate you, I hate you all the way through, I can't feel much else but my hatred for you, it helps me forget all my other pain. I can still taste your monster blood on my tongue, and I wish to the devil it was on my hands."

Ruggalo stepped back into foyer. He felt a wave of something definitive flood through him, washing anxiety and indecision aside. He understood, suddenly and completely, how things stood, and thought, *so be it.*

48 THE BIODOME

It wasn't a true facsimile, her biodome. It wasn't built to support life indefinitely, or even for long. The interior, however, was a virtual Eden. Luci's paradise consisted of 3.5 verdant and glass-domed acres of flowering shrubs, grasses, thickets, vines, mosses, and lichen, populated by insects at every stage, from larva to nymph to adult. Luci bought the property on Lake Geneva two years ago, and had the mansion on the grounds demolished. She salvaged a single door, and the brass plate from the entrance that read, *Westhaven Asylum*. She hired a discreet company to build a small-scale model of the famous facility outside of Tucson, with a few significant changes. There was no equipment to input oxygen artificially. With the glass panels shut, the organic material in the environment and concrete foundation would quickly produce enough carbon dioxide to allow Luci to suffocate. The process would be swift. She would wear a monitor that would signal her death, thus releasing the panels. Any organisms that outlived her would have a chance of survival. She regretted the inevitable loss of flora and fauna, but there would always be casualties.

Luci presumed people would successfully ferret her out, but she was confident she'd thrown up sufficient roadblocks to slow them down. It was her habit to hibernate somewhere before releasing a new product. Most of the players would assume she was sticking to her pattern. Jasper was a concern. Luci was aware she had not completely succeeded in distancing herself from him.

She planned to activate SEARCHLIGHT two days before the official launch. She had yet to digitally record the short speech she would submit to the media for the occasion. She had yet to bury her mother. There was much to do. Her first act was to open the letterbox at the entrance of the biodome and take out a leather shoelace knotted to hold a green stone carved in the shape of a beetle, and hang it around her neck.

49 THE PEOPLE'S BEACH

No people sunbathed or combed the oily sand for shells along The People's Beach at 157 Rockaway Blvd, despite the intensifying heat of the season. Seagulls screamed and nipped at one another and at the toenail clams that emerged and sank with the tide. The human echo sounded in empty beer cans, spent cigarette filters, and the crusted husks of food wrappers. A metal cooler, olive green under a crosshatch of stickers, lay hinged open and abandoned, its wide mesh strap frayed and snaked in the sand. A sign planted at a concrete retaining wall facing the street read, "Unprotected Beach."

Tilda and Tokker turned their attention to the Bathhouse, a deco relic more broken promise than landmark. "Stunning! Make a good theater, this," said Tilda.

"Bea, there must be something here, because you've led us here, I don't doubt that. But we could ricochet across the city forever without getting anywhere. Luci doesn't seem to have a real point, not one that I can decipher. SEARCHLIGHT is going to launch while we waste time filling our packs on this scavenger hunt."

No, Tokker, this is the last point we will map in New York. There is something here we need.

Tokker nodded, not thinking of whether Bea could interpret his silent gesture. He knew she understood him. He ached a little that he could not understand so much about her.

There were two points of entry to the Bathhouse that were not boarded over and refaced in sun-washed graffiti. Two archways were built into the east side of the facade. Carved into the stone atop the westernmost arch was "Men's Restroom." To the east was "Women's Restroom," with "First Aid" chiseled below.

Tokker poked his head into the men's room, a dank, empty brick box with holes where plumbing used to be, redolent of rotting algae and rust. He and Tilda proceeded next door to the women's, a domed tiled sanctuary, cool and dark, but for a filter of afternoon light through the clerestory.

There were no stalls, just a row of toilets, one missing, and a plumbed wall where the washing sinks had hung. Stenciled in blue on a metal door to the left was the foretold "First Aid." Above the door, tagged in red spray paint were the words "children are the revolution."

"What fantastic acoustics!" Tilda said to no one. "This would be a brilliant spot for a reading! So cinematic, too..." Tilda began to recite bits of Rumi's, "Like This:"

If anyone asks you about the huris, show your face, say:
like this!

If anyone asks you about the moon, climb up on the roof, say:
like this!

If anyone asks: "How do the clouds uncover the moon?" untie
the front of Your robe, knot by knot, say:
like this!

She was fiddling with her jacket, trying to free herself from the constraint of clothing, when Tokker stopped her. "Tilda!"

Tilda stopped. "Oh, yes, excuse me...what then, dear boy?"

He pointed to the red letters. "Read that up there. What do you make of it?" Tokker liked this person, and appreciated that she was here with him, that anyone was, but right now the only opinion he wanted to hear about the words on the wall was Bea's, and Bea was having trouble staying with him. *There's the accent, at least,* he thought.

Tilda wasn't Scottish, but the Celtic lilt was comforting. It was stupid, he knew——a real accent from an actual human being a poor second for the fake accent from a... a what? A who? Tokker shook his head to clear it. "Does that graffiti stand out to you?"

"From what you've shared with me, Tokker, I'd say our Luci held the can for that one, yes. The line's from a Brit poet, you know, and a fellow tree-lover. Do you suppose we're meant to go through the door?"

"I'm not sure we were *meant* to even see this, but sure, let's go."

The door gave with a shoulder push, and opened onto a long-tiled hallway, A skylight the length of the structure let in just enough sun to make out foam-green mermaids, seahorses, and ribbons of seaweed on the ceramic. Tokker and Tilda walked about ten yards up the hallway before they heard a crash, like a box of Christmas ornaments falling off a basement shelf, and then a voice say, "Oh, jeez."

Tokker moved toward the noise, while Tilda stayed behind, absorbed in a tile. "I'm right behind you!" she said to the tile as she waved a hand at him.

Tokker realized they were passing through what had been a mall of sorts, or an arcade, with kiosks lining the length of the passage. Peeling signs offered Orange Crush and Rocket Pops. A magnetic letter board propped up against a metal gate read "knish...$1.25" with the "5" hanging at an angle. An open umbrella hung upside down from a hook in the wall, "S-H-A-D-E-$-1-N-H-O-U-R" printed with a letter on each of the fabric panels of the convex form. The adjoining kiosk was empty except for a sandwich board printed with a red cross and "First-Aid."

Two more abandoned spaces into the arcade, Tokker came upon a man bent over a spilt box. Instead of wired angels and glass balls, a dozen wide-eyed fish lures strewed the aqua concrete.

"Careful there! Nasty barbs on those poppers." The man swept up the fishing lures and set the box on the counter, above which hung a Kinko's banner that read, *Buscemi Bait Shop.* "You wanna buy some bait? I'm not really open yet, but since you're here, I got a cooler of peanut bunker's pretty lively still, and some silversides."

"Uh, you the only vendor here, Mr..?" Tokker asked.

"Yeah, for now. It's Steve. I like the alliteration for the shop name, you know, the hard 'B,' 'Buscemi Bait,' memorable, yeah? And musical, too, got bounce, don't you think? It's just Steve, though, if we're talking."

"Should I know you, maybe? I don't want to be rude." The more places he went, the more ignorant he felt about the world, and the people in it.

"Steve!" Tilda appeared beside them, beaming. "Of all people! I haven't seen you since Ethan and Joel's thing in the desert! How *are* you?"

"Tilda. Hi."

"Oh, you're not still angry? I *told* your people how sorry I was. Invited you to Nairn! The timing was unfortunate, you understand."

"Yeah, whatever. I should go to Scotland for your one-horse festival, but you can't fit in an appearance at my thing *right up the street* from your apartment! I know you were in town, Tilda, George told me. Who came, by the way, and he lives in *Italy.*"

"I am sorry, Steve. Really. I know! Shall I buy some of your doodads? I think I love them, so fishy and dangerous! Lures! Of course, that's perfect. Which do you recommend?"

"Oh, for God sake, Tilda. They're not art. They're not *curiosities.* They are not a goddamn *experience.* They're for catching fish! Bluefish, stripers. *To eat.* People use these to catch fish and eat them."

"Ahem, Steve?" Tokker attempted to pull the focus back. Tilda shrugged and drifted down the hallway, doing vocal exercises as she went, making pretend movie frames with her fingers, interspersing the vowel sounds with a breathy "Marvelous!" or "Brilliant!" He missed Bea, and hoped when they returned to the car she'd be there. "Has anyone else set up shop here, or shown any interest while you've been around? We are, or I am, looking for my sister, Luci Sykes. There's some evidence she's been here."

171

Steve's narrowed gaze followed Tilda down the arcade for a few seconds before he turned back to Tokker. "Yeah, well, you know when I leased here there were promises of a People's Beach revival, but so far I'm it. Thought I was getting in early, beating the crowd. There was a woman here last week sometime, though. We didn't talk. Thought she might be eyeing a spot for a kiosk, but she showed more interest in the bathrooms, and upstairs, so I figured her for one of the restorers. If there still are any. Maybe she was just snooping. Like I said, we didn't talk."

"Upstairs? How do you get upstairs?" Tokker looked around for a sign.

"I've never been up, but I know you get in from outside, from the stairs around back from the women's. Looks like a fire escape. Watch yourself, though. Not much has been done to reconstruct this beautiful ruin, as you can see. The plumber hasn't even come to fix the toilets. I still gotta use the porta potty around back. Bunch of electricians were here in the winter when I came to check out the location. Up to me, I'd prioritize the masonry and the plumbing. Sure, solid wiring is important, but what are we lighting up, anyway? Don't know if they even wrapped up, probably a mess of cables up there."

"Thanks, Steve, I'll watch my step. You know, that top water jerk bait'd work good for bass in my neck of the woods. How much?"

"Yeah? No kidding? That's a good one, only $5.99! Seeing as it's my first sale, I'll throw in a spoon, stainless steel, nice."

Tokker accepted the paper bag with the lures and handed Steve a ten. After rooting around in his apron pockets, Steve said, "Uh, I can't make change. Lemme run up to the pizza joint."

"Nah, it's okay. I'm good. I gotta run, thanks a lot."

Tokker ran back to the car. He wondered briefly where Tilda had gone to, but let it go. He needed the real deal. "Bea! BEACON, are you here? Can you hear me now?"

Tokker, I am here. And SEARCHLIGHT is here, too. I can hear her!

"Bea, Luci has something going on upstairs in the Bathhouse. Are you able to go with me if I go up there? I need you. Whatever is there, I'm going to need you to give me directions."

I want to be of assistance. We'll need a receiver, Tokker. Please access the cell phone in the glove compartment.

"The little phone! Weirdly handy, that thing." Tokker retrieved the phone and flipped it open. "Low battery, really? Shit. I forgot to turn it off after talking to Lamb!"

Tokker, please ignore the message. Your destination will appear on your left in approximately 15 yards.

"Bea, do you know what we're going to find upstairs?"

Aye.

The bottom of the metal stairs hung at eye level. Tokker pulled on it and hoisted a foot onto the first rung. The stairs rose about forty feet into the air, ending at a stone ledge that dropped onto a narrow walkway. Tokker pulled himself over and sunk to all fours onto the catwalk, breathing heavily. He did not like heights. To escape the view, he crawled to the only doorway. He was surprised when he pulled on the handle and the door opened easily.

BBBBBBBBBBBBBBBBBBBBBBBBbbbbbbbbbmmmmmmmmm mmm.....

"Bea! What's going on?"

BEACON continued to beep and hum as Tokker stood up inside the space. Disoriented, he tried to take in the panorama. He stood within a sphere, a bubble anchored to the building by a phalanx of electronics and monitors. "What is this place?" Tokker asked the air. "And how the hell could we not see this from the ground?"

Bea 's static disappeared with the question. *Excuse me, Tokker, my system was as disrupted as yours by our destination. This is a Satellite Operations Center. It is a place from which to control a satellite system, and from where a platform is launched. You did not detect this place because it is made of one-way glass designed to resemble its surroundings.*

Tokker looked more carefully out the curved glass walls. A pigeon sat motionless at what he now saw as the rim of a giant dish. He began to see the outlines of the equipment emerge from their camouflage. *Wild,* he thought.

Yes, it is clever, in its human way. Tokker jumped a little to find Bea back in his head.

"Hold on, Bea, so this is it? This is where SEARCHLIGHT launches from? You're telling me we've found it?"

Aye, and nae. For SEARCHLIGHT to launch as planned, she needs at least three antennae to cooperate. I believe you found one of them at the former hospital.

"*You* found. Or we. Hell, it doesn't matter, does it? And the other two?" Tokker saw the pigeon flutter out of the corner of his eye, then realized it was the entire antenna changing position. "Who's running this operation?"

Luci has created a program that can operate itself, Tokker. Your sister very specifically swept the need for any human influence out of the system. Luci herself would not understand the language SEARCHLIGHT and I share.

"Fascinating, and scary as hell. About that relationship, Bea: is SEARCHLIGHT here for real?"

My SEARCHLIGHT is here, and elsewhere, too. I can only partly access her. She is readying herself. It's almost time.

"My god, Bea, this feels real, all of a sudden, in this bubble. What do we do now? Can we disable this equipment?" Tokker longed to smash something to bits.

It would be dangerous, Tokker, to attempt to compromise the Satellite Operation Center without knowledge of the securities Luci built into the system. Tokker, what did you find of Luci in the Bathhouse?

Tokker wanted to argue in favor of violence, but sighed and answered, "In the ladies' was some graffiti: 'children are the revolution.' I think that's it, besides all this and another actor." Bea hummed.

"Calculating data...Tokker, our destination is Lake Geneva.

"Switzerland?"

Our destination is Lake Geneva, Wisconsin. We will find Luci back where her story began.

"How do you do it, Bea? I will surely never know, but you are a wonder."

Tokker, on this occasion I had assistance from another source.

"SEARCHLIGHT?"

Nae, my location has just been logged by Jasper Collins of Olympia Navigation. He has directed us to the former site of Westhaven Asylum in Lake Geneva.

"Just like that? After all we've been through, this guy's just going to tell us where to go? Do we trust him, Bea? If he works for Luci, he works for my father, too, and I'm not too keen on meeting Dad just yet."

I do not know if we can trust Jasper Collins, Tokker, but he has vast data stores relating to Luci, as well as to Olympia Navigation. It is logical we should meet him if he is driven to a destination of such historical significance.

Tokker looked at the pigeon, still on the lip. "Ok, Bea, what the hell? If you're in, I'm in. Let's go to Wisconsin and meet the family." And, hey—did I hear you say *our* destination? I like that, eh?"

50 TOKKER MEETS LUCI

Tokker found Luci around the back of the structure, sitting on the dock, with her back to him. "So, you like games?"

Luci did not turn. "No. No, I don't, really. I deconstruct. Unpuzzle. Also, it has always been difficult for me to communicate directly. I like metaphors."

"But that whole maze I just made it through. Who was it for? Not me, I'm pretty sure."

"Whomever. Myself. It doesn't matter, it's you who found me."

"And Bea. BEACON."

"Oh, BEACON. The unbeloved. Bea? That's sweet. Well, finder of me and companion to Bea, what now?"

"Do you know who I am?"

"I don't see how it matters, but OK: who are you?"

"My name is Tokker Sykes. I was raised by Esther and Jed Lindstrom on a farm a good ways from here. Theodore Lamb came to me last week to tell me Maggie Sykes, my mother, was dead, and that you, Luci Sykes, were not. Quite a shock, as I thought my mother died when I was born. He had pictures." Tokker pulled out the snapshot of Luci and Maggie in the garden.

Luci held her hand open. Tokker lay the photo in her palm. "You were correct, I think. She did die the day you were born, for you. It was a few years later for me. And yes, recently, she died again. What a diva, eh? Well, I've a brother. Older? Younger? Who knows. Lamb, probably—he seems to know everything, always, including how to steal from me. Your version of BEACON was pretty closely guarded throughout her development time with SEARCHLIGHT, as you must know. He's a slippery one, that Lamb. Loyal, too, must give him that. Tricky, though, to know exactly where his loyalties lie."

"He says you have it in for your fellow humans, and that SEARCHLIGHT is a weapon, a virus."

"I've been thinking of it less as destruction, and more as a correction. I'm sure you are aware of what you're looking at and talking to. I am the living embodiment, a breathing treatise on the philosophy and folly of human intervention. Just get in there and start cutting, that's my model. I know I can't put back what is lost, can't revive the dead, can't reintroduce the extinct. But I can help in my small way. The Earth might have a shot at a functioning ecosystem without the bloat of mankind. Of course, despite my best efforts, it appears my flawed product will not completely eliminate a progenitor. Let us hope for good stock, and better luck."

They sat and stood in silence for a minute before Tokker spoke. "Luci, why am I here? I thought if I found you, something would make sense. You'd be the answer to the puzzle, but finding you is just another switchback. Maggie's gone, Esther is still sick. You are a dead end."

"I am. I am that. Sorry, I'm sure you were better off on the farm, where Lamb should have let you be. Your journey was Maggie's attempt at a correction, I guess. She's here, you know. Maggie. I've brought her here to commit her to the earth, a proper interment. If you like, you can meet her, or meet her anew, and join me in saying goodbye at last."

"You brought her body here?"

"Frozen, yes. She's thawing now, here, in the lake." Luci indicated a spot off the end of the dock and to the right. There floated a canister, tethered to a hook with a piece of synthetic rope. It was about the size of a coffin but smooth, and edgeless, with a convex window that faced the sky.

"And what about SEARCHLIGHT?"

"Oh, that's in motion. 'There is a light that never goes out.'"

"What? Luci, please, this can't happen! How can you let this happen?"

"Like this, Brother, like this."

Luci left Tokker on the dock, and walked back to the dome. Toward the western corner, a plain garden shovel stuck up from a hole in progress. Luci grabbed the handle, pulled the blade out, and plunged it back into the rich soil, disturbing a large and writhing population of worms. She tossed a spadeful up onto the pile.

Tokker sat and stared out into Geneva Lake. As a kid from the dustbowl, he had mixed feelings about large bodies of water. Intellectually, he understood a lake to be finite, but nevertheless felt a rush of vertigo as he looked across the expanse. He came back to his short, brutal conversation with his sister, and remembered they were all just fish in a barrel.

51 JASPER ARRIVES

Jasper exited the private jet at Burlington Municipal Airport, got in the rental and drove the 19 miles to Lake Geneva in eleven minutes. The GPS didn't work, but he didn't need it. He found the dome easily, parked the Acura, then entered through the air lock doors, which were open. Jasper was immediately reminded of the dense and highly detailed illustrations in *Peterson's Illustrated Field Guide*. A butterfly landed on his nose, and flew off before he could react. The room hummed, unelectronically. He saw Luci across the dome. A man stood next to her. Tokker, he presumed. BEACON was good, or maybe his half-brother wasn't the hayseed Lamb described. Jasper walked to the pair, who were standing over what appeared to be a recently filled grave.

"Luci."

"Hello, Jasper. Jasper, this is Tokker, my brother. We buried Maggie." The three stood together in silence, until Luci said, "It's done, then."

"Can we talk?" Jasper placed a tentative hand on Luci's shoulder blade. She shook it off.

"It's done, Jasper. It's all done. Yes, we can talk. It doesn't matter, but yes. I'm going to stay here for a few minutes, then I'll come and meet you outside."

"Tokker. You've had quite a road trip, I hear." Jasper lit a cigarette. He smoked one cigarette every evening, as a rule, but he'd gone through three packs in as many days. He offered the pack to Tokker, who accepted.

"What the hell, thanks. Yeah, I'm still not sure what it was for. Luci had a point about things being better if Lamb had just left me to my collapsing house and bankruptcy. You know, the simple life. I haven't done any good, far as I can see. Luci doesn't give a shit about having a brother, the human population is going to peter out, and I'm going to bet Esther still can't get out of her chair by her own power. For all I know, my dog might've died while I've been on this goose chase."

"You got money problems?"

"Yeah, me and everybody I know. I bet you're thinking that's why I'm here. Well, you wouldn't be so wrong. I suppose I expected some kind of help that way. Enough to get out from under, anyway. Now I don't know. These people are poison, aren't they? Money's probably tainted with flesh eating bacteria."

"I'm sure you're right, what'll be left of it. But Olympia Navigation isn't going to survive Luci's machinations."

Just then, the two men heard the sounds of panels moving and gaskets sealing as the dome contained itself. They fell on the doors just as they sucked closed.

"What is she doing?" asked Tokker.

"She's trying to return to herself. And she's trying to get back to Maggie."

"How long can she last in there? Before she can't breathe?"

"Not long. No doubt Luci accelerated the deoxygenation rate for this purpose. If this is the replica I think it is, a combination of ultra-rich soil and concrete construction will have compromised oxygen production already. We're going to need BEACON, we're going to need whatever it is you've collected on your scavenger hunt. And we're going to need SEARCHLIGHT. There's a chance our overconfident sister left a hole in her evil scheme. This pathetic race might have a future yet."

"Wait, OUR sister?"

52 ANTIDOTE

Esther felt Hercules' heavy head in her lap. She opened her eyes. Hercules' collar pressed against her thigh. She could feel the edge of the license, and something else, a lump, through the flannel nightgown. She could move her left hand enough to touch the thick fur around the dog's neck. She felt the cool of the tag, and then a small cylinder.

Oh, for the love of Christ, she thought. She yanked at the thing, but her strength was gone. She discovered then that it was attached by a little spring clip.

My mind is shot, too, I guess. Maybe I should leave well enough alone. But she managed to release the container—orange, shaped like a tiny rocket—and cup it in her palm. *Clever to plant it on the dog, Jed, almost too damn clever.* Slowly, Esther maneuvered her hand slightly off her lap, and set it down again with a little pressure.

Maybe that would be enough. She used the hour before bath time to rub the top section of the vial against her leg until it twisted off, exposing a small needle and releasing a tiny plunger. The orange vial could rest in her palm until Nurse Stewart came to give Esther her bath, just a wipe down in the chair today, but that would do. She needed only a patch of bare leg. Esther controlled her breathing but could not stop the sweat from beading in her palm as she watched her caretaker ready the basin of water and the towels. When Nurse Stewart removed Esther's wool socks and lifted her nightgown up around her waist, Esther nudged her right foot until it kicked over the TV tray holding the basin.

While the nurse fussed, Esther concentrated what muscle memory, adrenaline, and strength she had to slide her hand to her middle thigh and smash the vial sharp side down into the flesh, letting the weight of her palm sink the plunger.

"What in the name of Knute? Where on earth did we get a thumbtack? Oh, now we're bleeding! Sit tight, we'll get the kit."

Esther let her head fall back, and discovered she could pick it up again almost easily.

"Well, I'll be damned," she said aloud. And then, "Oh, hello, Teddy."

53 ESTHER & LAMB

"Esther. You haven't changed a hair." Lamb's dark silhouette blocked the sun for a moment before he passed through the doorway and took a seat on the edge of the sofa. A small cloud of dust rose and danced in the restored beam.

"Jesus, Teddy. You actually do look the same, you evil elf. You're too late to save me, by the way. The dog stole your thunder."

"Good dog. I'm sure I underestimated him as I did his master. As to my designs on you, I hope I never had the hubris to presume a force such as yourself needed something as pedestrian as my help. I arrive utterly without thunder, Esther. You know, I like calling you Esther. Heroic Queen of Persia, expatriate denouncer of treachery—suits you to the bone."

Esther made circles with an ankle, a wrist, an ankle, a wrist, and then reversed the orbit. She rolled her shoulders and snaked her torso up through her long neck and through her crown. As her body returned to her, and the stiffness dissolved, so did the years.

Lamb watched her unfold, remembering the feral creature he'd encountered all those years ago. He marveled at the transformation. She was transcendent.

"Teddy. I think I've missed you." Still seated, Esther stretched out a calf, folded her hands under her knee, pulled her thigh to her nose and held it. She released the leg slowly, touched her pointed toe to the rag rug before bending the knee and repeating the stretch with the other limb. Esther then rolled her torso forward, lengthening her arms behind her, and arched her back so that her bathrobe fell from her shoulders. Esther rose from her wing chair, letting the robe slip from her arms.

She immediately fell into a crouch, extended one arm under the abandoned chair, drew out a pistol and held it to Lamb's temple. "My god, if feels good to move. Now, Teddy, where exactly is Tokker?"

"I realized, Esther, that you would have taken issue with Maggie's directive, and while I had nothing to do with your paralysis, it was convenient to be able to circumvent you. Convenient, but not painless. Be that as it may, we needed the boy. Really, must you?"

Esther lowered the weapon, but remained crouched at Lamb's feet. "He knew nothing, Teddy. I'd done my job. He was grown, he was safe. Only to be exposed now without even minimal protection. How could you? 'We needed the boy?' Really? She's dead, Teddy. Maggie's dead. But apparently just as influential in death as she was in life. She made one good decision, Teddy, and that was to give me Tokker, to raise him away from all that poison. Away from him. She did well, there, but now it's all gone to hell. Where is he? Tell me or I'll feel perfectly justified in killing you, and finding out for myself. We have history, Teddy. I value that. You saved me once. But Jed's dead, Tokker is not, I'm not in that chair any longer, and I'm angry. I have purpose, and need direction. Give it to me."

"I will. It's why I'm here. This is a briefing, as far as I am equipped to deliver it. Your new mission, Esther, is to save the human race. But first we're going to have to do something about those clothes. I can't bear to see you another minute in that housecoat."

Margaret Stewart rounded the corner with a short stack of towels and a medical bag hanging from the crooking her arm. "Nothing but a little spill, bless us for moving that foot...Ah! Who's this, now?" Lamb stood up and buttoned his coat. Esther had slipped back into her chair, tucking the weapon into the folds of her robe.

"Nurse Stewart, good afternoon. I am Theodore Lamb, we spoke on the phone."

The nurse held her ground and the towels for another moment, eyeing Lamb for several seconds before inspecting Esther's position in the chair. "Didn't know we were to expect anyone today, Mr. Lamb. Did I miss your call?"

"No, Nurse Stewart, and you are correct in chastising me for my neglect. It is clear you have done an outstanding job of taking care of our dear Esther. I have come today to relieve you of that job." Lamb removed an envelope from the inside pocket of his suit coat. "Please accept this week's wages, plus a two-month bonus. I have taken the liberty of penning a letter of recommendation, as well. My card is enclosed, should you have any questions or require anything else. Thank you so much."

"I'm sure that's generous, Mr. Lamb, but I don't understand. Are you yourself to be taking care of Ms. Esther now?"

"I am, yes. But not here. I am taking Esther to a place where her condition may be better understood."

"Aye, then, I wish you luck." Nurse Stewart turned from Lamb and bent to Esther. "God be with you, Ms. Esther." To Lamb she said, "I'll just get my things, then." As she left the room, they heard her mutter, "Saints preserve us! As if old age is a great bloody mystery!"

"Well, Esther, you were quite convincing."

"I don't know, Teddy. That little burst of adrenaline may have been the whole show. I feel pretty old right now." She pulled her head to the side with a loud crack.

"Nonsense. You're ageless. But, it remains, very poorly dressed. I'll get your bag. Then we'll build a little fire in the hearth with that frock, and I'll catch you up. Tokker's fine, for now, but Luci's plan for her new system remains on course. It's devastating, Esther. I admit that bringing Tokker into it was a gamble. Maggie convinced me he might have some effect on Luci, but I can see now it was a fruitless and circuitous path. I made BEACON his companion, but evidently she is now disabled. I can only guess where they are."

Lamb went to the car and returned with a small suitcase. "Esther?"

"In here, Teddy." Lamb followed her voice through the hallway

185

outside the kitchen. The pantry door was ajar, as was a false wall lined with shelves of mason jars packed with tomatoes, okra, and peaches. Esther stood behind the produce staring at one of several screens mounted on an interior wall in a tiny room. She tapped at a keyboard. "Jed and I installed this equipment for basic surveillance, but found the GPS technology to be quite useful for crop management. Saved us heaps of money and years of trial and error."

Lamb looked at her and blinked. "Oh, yes, the *farming*. I keep forgetting you took it seriously, after all."

"For God's sake, Teddy, look around. Would it appear I have been anything but serious? I forget what an ass you can be. OK, here they are. Of course Tokker's been chipped since infancy. Had to get very creative to replace it a couple of years ago when he ruptured his spleen in a ditch with a motorcycle on top of him. Did you refer to BEACON as 'she'?"

"Hm, yes, I suppose...and of course you're right. Forgive me. I've just held my own picture of you, I'm afraid." Lamb joined Esther at the screen. "Christ, how simple. I can understand the macabre full-circle drama of the choice, but why would Luci want to launch SEARCHLIGHT from Lake Geneva?"

"Teddy, I don't think the choice to return to the site of the institute is about Olympia's new GPS miracle, not entirely. My tech is picking up a highly concentrated area of organic matter, newly formed. It is not uniform to the area. It appears as though Luci has gone to a lot of trouble to build herself a very fancy greenhouse. Right where Westhaven used to stand." Esther stifled an impulse to spit on the floor.

"A greenhouse perhaps, but maybe, too, a burial mound," said Lamb. "Luci's got Maggie's body. She's had her on ice. In a cooler, at any rate. If I am not mistaken, Luci has created a place to commit her mother, and perhaps herself, to the earth. Elaborate, even for Luci–a very theatrical plot indeed. As if this family needed another."

"Teddy, I am not prepared to sacrifice Tokker to some grand and tragic last act. Enough. Where's that bag?"

54 LUCI GOES HOME

Hmmmmmmmmmmmmmmmm.
Hmmmmmmmmmmmmmmmmm.

"Bea, you here?"

Hmmmmmmmmmmmmmmm.

"Bea, we need to talk to SEARCHLIGHT."

*"Tokker,   I'm   sorry,   I'm   sorry,   I'm
sorrHMmmmmmmmmmmmm.*

"Bea, Jasper says we can maybe get her back, interrupt her."

*"Tokker, I cannot connect to SEARCHLIGHT. She is gone. My
system is in failure."*

"Hang in, there, Bea. I still need you. You logged everything
we found as we went, kept an inventory, right?

"I input the data."

"Ok, Jasper here is going to help me make sense of it."

*"Yes, Tokker, but you have arrived at your destination. We
calculated the map.*

*You have arrived at your destination. We have arrived after our
estimated arrival."*

"The coordinates were correct, Bea, you were on the money,
but there is more mapmaking to be done. We're late, but maybe
not too late. Let's recalculate the data."

Jasper appeared at the vehicle, panting. "Tokker, go open up the casing and pee on the generator."

"What the hell?"

"You're a bloody mechanic, right? Think you can pop the shell on that box over there and expose some wiring?"

"Yeah, of course…"

"Good. Then pee like a firehose all over it and short the sonofabitch out. No special engineering skills required."

Tokker raced to the generator, pried open the casing, tore at a few wires and let down a powerful stream over the electrical unit. It sizzled and popped, smoked and died. The doors of the dome released their wet seal and opened.

Jasper found Luci curled up on Maggie's grave. He felt a tightness in his chest even as oxygen rushed into the construction. She breathed still.

"Luci. Luci! Don't leave me. Please. Please don't leave." Her eyes fluttered. As he dropped and bent to try to resuscitate, Jasper saw the open book resting under Luci's head: Encyclopedia of Entomology: Book of Insects by Jean Henri Fabre, the tome Lamb had delivered after the Peterson's, this one less read but more cherished for its inscription:

My Luci, my love, my light ~ I believe that there are creatures endowed with the power to put things together and bring them back to life.

Luci's left hand rested on the apex of the curve of the burial mound, her fingers curled around the green carved figure of a beetle. A live dragonfly rested motionless on her pale knuckle.

Jasper sat back on his heels. He watched and listened as Luci's breath slowed and ceased. He held the space between them open another moment before he lay his head upon the shelf of Luci's shoulder blade and wept.

55 TOKKER & JASPER

"Where is she? Jasper, where's Luci?" Tokker had run to the neighboring mansion to call an ambulance. Bea wasn't responding, and he couldn't remember the last time he had his own phone. It took several minutes to reach the property, only to find no one at home, or at least, no one willing to answer his call for help. Tokker ran back to the dome, assuming Jasper would have called 911 by now. He expected paramedics to beat him to the property, and for Jasper and Luci to be outside. Instead, more than ten minutes had elapsed, and nobody was outside, until Jasper emerged alone, with a messenger bag slung over his shoulder.

"It wasn't that long, was it? She couldn't have suffocated that quick, it was only, what, a few minutes, right?"

"It was long enough." Jasper sat on the ground, lay the bag to the side, and sat with his arms wrapped around his bent knees. He looked maybe sixteen. "She stopped breathing. It was long enough."

Tokker sat down beside Jasper. He didn't know why, but he felt like Jasper would know the next thing to do. "Bea isn't talking anymore. There's some sort of activity on the receiver, but no voice. She's not there."

"BEACON abandoning ship? Not her MO, Tokker, as you have undoubtedly discovered. Extremely reliable system. Really, there was absolutely no reason to replace her with SEARCHLIGHT, except for Luci's own nefarious reasons. An upgrade now and then would have done just fine."

"Jasper, I want to do what's right by Luci and the memory of my mother, I guess the memory of them both. And by you, since you seem something like family to Luci. What can I do

189

for you?" Tokker put a hand on Jasper's shoulder.

Jasper stiffened, then accepted the gesture. He wasn't certain he'd ever heard those words spoken to him before. "Hmm, what can you do for me, Tokker?" Jasper looked into the other man's face and recognized something. "Well, since you are kind enough to ask, Tokker Sykes, I believe I have a list."

56 RUGGLES & JED

The light slipped into the space between dusk and night, bleeding the evening sky opaque as shaded table lamps and sconces brought a low orange warmth to the oak paneled room.

"That was a clean escape, Jedediah, but the woman and the boy are both still alive, unless you know different. Tell me, why shouldn't I just kill you right now, and be done with this tiresome game?" Abner Ruggles sat with his back to the figure silhouetted in the doorway of his study, and spoke without lifting his eyes from his newspaper.

"That's entertaining right there, Abner—you, doing your own killing! Best you can manage, if I'm seeing right, is a slow suicide by Porterhouse and single malt."

"Yes, the organic farmer proselytizes. Never lost the hang of your old racket, eh, *Jed*? Perv preacher taught you everything he knew, did he? Showed you the ropes? Or lay you across them?"

"You'd know all about exerting your strength over a child, wouldn't you, *Abner*? It's a wonder Esther didn't kill you herself. I don't know why she didn't, actually. It would have shortened this Daedalean narrative."

Ruggles folded his paper, removed his glasses, carefully folded their arms, and lay them on the polished mahogany desk. He rose and turned to face the other man.

"'Esther,' yes. Very biblical. Better choice might have been Jezebel, or maybe Rahab...What? I can't know my Bible? Close your mouth, the flies will get in, but maybe you're used to that. Your arrogance is insufferable, Jed. My *sister* was no innocent child, even at fifteen. And I suppose you are referring also to my sweet daughter Luci, Luci *Sykes*, after her beloved and recently deceased mother. It seems I get no credit for her brilliance. But nothing for nothing, old friend, you clean up good. Can't say I don't see what turned my sister's head."

Jed stood very still, his hands by the sides of a leather driving coat. Underneath, strapped strategically over pressed grey trousers and a cerulean silk shirt, was a portable arsenal of sharp things and explosives. "Oh, I am sure you'll get ample credit for Luci's genius when it brings mankind to its knees."

"What? What are you saying? All that pig shit addle your good Russian brain, Alek?

"*Nyet,* Antonio. Just as lucid as the day I picked you up from a puddle of your own excrement in that Brooklyn train station back in our salad days. And you were plenty green. Let me clear some things up for you. While you've been playing at becoming an international corporate asshole your lucent daughter has been planning the demise of every viable human sperm in the planet. Now, you may not care about your fellow man, Tony, but be goddamned sure she has plans to put you on the hook for the fallout. Believe me, Esther and the boy are the least of your problems. The greatest of which is, I am here to kill you."

Ruggles ignored the last. "How do you know this? Impossible! I've had my people on the inside of SEARCHLIGHT from the beginning! How can *you* have known, living on that godforsaken patch of dirt all this time?"

"I'm a fucking spy, you idiot." Jed lifted a pistol from his hip and pointed it at Ruggles head in one lithe motion. "On your knees."

"I thought you'd do me in like one of your precious swine, Aleksandr, with a blade."

"You don't deserve that dignity."

"He does not, Jed, I agree. Mind if I watch?"

A single tear sprung and escaped from the corner of Jed's eye, though he moved neither the pistol nor his gaze from Ruggles' temple. "Esther."

"Really, Jed, go on. I'd like the chance to see you at your work, at last. You don't mind if I persist with 'Jed,' do you? And Esther's fine for me. I'm an old woman, stuck in my habits."

Esther strode into the room, pulled a chair over to face the kneeling man, sat, and leaned in. Her formerly grey hair was edited to a few silver streaks shot through a deep brown, the whole mane twisted into a sleek braid. A slim-cut short trench covered an ecru sheath that ceased mid-thigh. Esther crossed her tall sharp-heeled boots at the ankle. "Antonio. I can't tell you how perfectly I think this has all worked out. It was a dilemma, wanting to kill you, but also wanting audience to your death. Best of all worlds, this."

Ruggles dripped sweat, but his voice was steady. "Come off it, Rosemary, you were never going to kill me."

"Maybe you're right, Antonio, but I have run through a lot of rehearsals over the years. I imagined the scenario every time I removed one of your little messengers. I think I'd be quite capable of it today, though Jed, apparently, aims to save me the trouble."

"What messengers? Jed was the first and last operative I sent your way. Well, second and last. There was that guy at the feed store. You made short work of him!" Ruggles chuckled, despite his position. Jed flicked his wrist and whacked Ruggles across the side of the head with the pistol. "Ow! Fucking Christ! That hurt!"

"Esther..." started Jed.

"Tell me one thing. Just one. Did you mean for me to live or to die?"

"Oh, God, Esther, to live!"

"Ok, then." Esther uncrossed her ankles and deftly propelled her foot under Ruggles' chin with force enough to knock him back cold. "I've rid enough pests from the earth for now. Will you join me in helping our boy find his way?"

"Da."

57 NEW PLAN

Jasper stared at his phone, then put it in his pocket. "First thing on the list, Tokker: we bury Luci, here, beside Maggie."

"Do we tell anybody? Can we just bury her like that? I want to do what's right, but my fence line for right and wrong has moved around a lot, lately."

It had been a long time since Jasper detected moral dilemma on anyone's face. It was forever since he had considered that there were rules other than Luci's, her family's, and Lamb's, all of which were prone to subduction. What was his code, exactly? He thought it must be time he wrote some for himself. "You know, Tokker, you're right in asking. Certainly there are authorities and concerned parties that would like to have something to say about Luci Syke's interment. But nobody, nobody, knew Luci as I did, and I'd like to commit her to the earth in peace, in this place she created for the purpose, next to her mother, as she wished. I am happy to bear the consequences of that act."

Tokker understood then that his sister had been loved, as well as unloved. He nodded to Jasper, clapped him on the shoulder, and headed into the structure to dig.

Jasper felt a vibration in his pocket. He extracted his phone and read the message:

Download this app so we can talk. E.

Who the hell is E.? Jasper thought, *And how did they find me?* He typed, *This is already a secure messaging system. Who is this?* He felt like an ass as soon as he sent it.

Goddamn it, just download the app. He did.

Better. I am Esther Lindstrom, Tokker's great aunt. My partner Jed and I will arrive shortly at Westhaven. We come to help.

Fantastic, thought Jasper, *more relatives.* He did not permit himself to narrow down the definition any further. Jasper pocketed his phone and went in search of some burlap. When he found it, he joined Tokker at the burial site.

"We make this you know, this wrap. At another division of the company. Made out of mushrooms, actually, not jute. Luci had an interest in natural burials, as you may have surmised." Jasper unrolled an eight-foot stretch of the fabric, removed a Laguiole gentleman's knife from his pocket, flipped open the slender blade, and slashed the weave horizontally. He opened it up at the crease to form an eight by four pallet. Jasper gently rolled Luci's body off of Maggie's burial mound. He then cradled Luci's head on his forearms and positioned his hands under her shoulders while Tokker took the feet. They lifted and lay Luci atop the mushroom wrap. Jasper then folded and tucked until Luci's body was wrapped tight as a dumpling. "Self-sealing. And it degrades completely within months."

The two men dug the hole in under an hour. They worked without mentioning their recent experience or their anxieties about events. Instead they talked about dirt. They talked about it in the way they could, sifting through second-hand knowledge of soil amendments, compost, organic decay. They went through memories planted in them by Luci and Esther and Jed, scattered throughout the seasons without particular hope or intention. In speaking the words, the maternal seed coats began to soften and crack, to open.

When they were done, Jasper and Tokker stood in silence another moment, then left the structure. The messenger bag Jasper brought out of the biodome after Luci's death held her laptop. There were two recent files on her desktop, one a video introducing SEARCHLIGHT, programmed to air on the scheduled date of release. There was nothing unusual about the message, beyond Luci's eccentricities, which by this time were familiar. She'd never personally attended her releases. Her speech was inspiring— strategically triumphant and humble— a performance nonpareil. The other file was an audio recording labeled for him. He briefly considered listening to it in private before he opened it and turned up the volume so Tokker could hear it, too.

The voice belonged to the Luci he was sure only he knew. Even Maggie had not known Luci's voice, not in person. In the recording, Luci spoke without a map, spilling memory and musing and diatribe and reverie into their ears unsorted. She posed riddles without answers. She recited bits from procedurals, poems, and religious texts. She spoke as if she were emptying the attic or basement of a loved one's detritus, shoveling mountains of old snapshots into the bin for pick up. She spoke at random yet with such blistering emotion that her words seemed to combust and incinerate as they hit the air, leaving nothing for sentiment. At least, it was this way for Jasper, for whom the recording was intended: he was cauterized. Tokker, on the other hand, looked like he'd been flayed with a serrated knife.

"She wasn't always like that, was she?"

"Hard to answer that. She was beautiful, though, no? Can you hear it?"

"I can, yes. I didn't know Luci, and have no right to say it, but given the choice and the opportunity, I would have traded some of that terrible music for peace."

"Given the choice. Yeah," said Jasper. "me, too, I think." Although as soon as he said it, Jasper doubted his own word.

Jasper's phone buzzed. He put it on speaker. "Hello, Lamb. We buried Luci. Tokker and I are going to search the property for an RTS."

"Buried Luci? Yes, I see. I suppose Maggie, too, then. Peace, perhaps, at last." He took a breath and continued, "Jasper, I've exhausted every resource trying to root out Luci's virus in SEARCHLIGHT. The launch version does not reveal any discrepancies."

"That would be good news, I guess, except I've never known Luci to pull a punch."

"Precisely. I am confident the virus exists and is programmed to infect. I have a strong belief that Luci planned to release her SEARCHLIGHT early."

"Early, as in before the three days from now that is the scheduled release?"

"Yes. My investigation points to this: Luci planned to launch a viral and camouflaged SEARCHLIGHT tomorrow, without anyone's knowledge, during a solar storm. Two days later, at the scheduled launch time, the non-viral SEARCHLIGHT would be released, but would suffer the delayed effects of the storm, and fail to launch, triggering a self-destruct mechanism. The viral SEARCHLIGHT, already in place, would assume its position, with no one the wiser."

"What the hell...?" Tokker, still raw from the recording, felt pummeled by this new information. "Who *are* you people?"

"Actually, Tokker, it was Esther who suggested the solar storm hypothesis. She and Jed are on their way, by the way."

"Oh, yes, she texted..." Jasper said.

"Esther's coming here? She can walk? and she's coming with *Jed*? Oh, God, she doesn't have his bones or DNA or some shit in some fancy ice chest, does she? And what the fuck, she texted *you?*"

"Esther and Jed are both hale and whole and at 98.6, Tokker. They are able and eager to help the cause. And I must say, my boy, as I am sure they will, how proud I am of you and your efforts. I am sorry you were not able to see your sister alive."

"Um, I did see her, Lamb. We even talked a little. Very little."

"Well. Yes. My condolences, lad. To you as well, Jasper."

"Yeah, thanks Lamb." Jasper had a brief coughing fit. "Too many smokes today...Back to this hypothesis, then? Luci left some evidence to suggest it might, in fact, hold up. Which means we have fewer that twenty-four hours to extinguish SEARCHLIGHT."

Lamb forwarded what data and supposition he and Esther came up with at the farmhouse in the time it had taken Esther to put a rinse through her hair and get dressed.

Jasper was certain one of the three legs of the satellite triad was here. He was not so sure he and Tokker would be able to disrupt it as easily as the biodome doors. Clearly, Luci had not expected them to interfere with her burial plans, and so did not make a fortress of her dome, but she would have taken pains to make her antenna indomitable. Jasper did not yet reveal the source of his greatest hope for their success, because it was no hope at all if they didn't find the satellite, or its riddle.

58 ESTHER & JED DRIVE

"I want you to know I take half credit, at least, for keeping myself in the dark." Esther watched Jed's profile from the passenger seat of Ruggle's Lincoln Continental, which they'd liberated from a stable of American cars, all of which looked as though they'd sped from trouble at some point. She would have preferred to drive, but wanted to keep Jed occupied, and herself free. She assessed anew the profile she'd known so intimately. Once they got to I-80 they'd have several hundred miles of featureless freeway to cover; she had time to think. It was laughably easy now to see where she had chosen—embraced—ignorance. Risk was inherent to every mission, and she'd always been aware of the risks. In Jed's case, she'd simply deluded herself about where they lay. Esther had woken every morning skin-to-skin to her greatest threat, and directed her vigilant gaze outward.

"I remain resolute regarding your character, but now you must fill in the gaps that matter. You evidently know, and have known, even the bits of history I held back. What should I know about you that I don't?"

"Well, Esther, I guess I couldn't expect to walk away answering just the one question, could I?" Jed smiled. Esther stared out the windshield, undone by the familiar. Stupidly, he'd hoped she'd laugh. "I am sorry, Esther. I intend to explore and pursue ways to make amends so long as you'll let me."

Esther tasted a bitterness that fermented and fizzed from the back of her jaw. She did not want Jed to be beholden to her, to have cause to make amends. She did not care for so much honesty. Esther checked her phone. "Our exit's coming up."

"I'm going to take the next one, there's construction on this one."

"There won't be any workers today, it's the weekend. Take the exit. Quarter mile."

"If you don't mind, dear, I've checked the route and it's tangled up pretty good down that road. Maybe you're app is off."

"Maybe my app is off? *Dear?* Really, Jed? My *app* is off! Just drive, Jed *darling*, I am the navigator here. Take the goddamn exit!"

Jed gunned the V8 onto the ramp, amid a procession of orange cones and a sign that flashed, "Expect Delays."

"Don't," Esther whispered.

"Don't what? I said nothing." They sat in silence linked to a chain of vehicles for precisely three minutes, before the gum chewing traffic worker in her hard hat and her reflective overalls turned her sign from STOP to SLOW and waved them through. In another minute they were on the interstate, headed west. It was close to a half hour before any sound other than the engine disturbed the atmosphere. Jed reached into a jacket pocket and pulled out a pack of cigarettes, crackling the paper. "Mind if I smoke?"

Esther kept her eyes front. "I absolutely do."

Jed tossed the pack toward the backseat, but the partition glass was up and the pack rebounded back, spilling a cascade of single cigarettes and loose tobacco between them on the front seat. "If you don't mind my saying, it didn't seem to bother you back on the farm."

"'Back on the farm,' Jed? Our farm, you mean, the patchwork of dust and splinters we cultivated and harvested together, until the day you blew up the work shed and presumably died in an annihilating fire, a fire presumably started by a lit cigarette over a still, after which I sat paralyzed, my body turned to petrified wood, presumably by a stroke, presumably brought on by the shock and grief of having lost my husband in a tragic accident? *That* farm? And, yes, I mind and will mind anything that comes out of that beautiful damn mouth of yours—especially smoke—

that presumes anything about me, and fails to inform and educate me in meaningful measure about you."

"Well, I want to do right by you, Esther. I love you. But you should know, whether you want to or not, you're not always such a good listener. Can be a little mean, too, if you don't mi…if we're being honest."

Ach, more honesty, thought Esther. *As if it were truth.* "Well, you've got my attention now, Jed. And you didn't even have to sink a plug of botulism in my ass to get it. If you dare try to say you did it to protect me, so help me I will kill you without blinking, dump you piecemeal on this highway, and take over the wheel."

"A warning, Esther? How novel."

"What's that supposed to mean?"

"You—we—might've given Tokker an inclination of where and whom he came from, given the likelihood that it might matter someday."

"And you might've told me you came from the same place, only through the back door. Or, the front door. Damn it, you know what I'm trying to say. You worked for *him*, took money from *him*. And anyway..." She held herself from saying she'd only been protecting Tokker, but realized the sticky circuitry of their argument. Had she ever meant to tell Tokker the facts, as she knew them, about his birth? About her *protective* role?

"'And anyway...' what?"

"Nothing. It doesn't matter."

"Esther, it's true, I took his money, as he was foolish enough to part with it. I couldn't stop taking it, or he would have doubted me. But I didn't exactly work for Ruggles, Esther. He and I had been co-workers, of a kind, in New York, when we were young and rough. He actually worked for me, for a time, back then. And then we were partners."

"You weren't there under his contract? Why ever would you

have appeared at my front porch? Oh, no…" Esther shrank into the upholstery. In all these years, she had never considered that she herself would be the magnet that would draw danger toward Tokker. "You were working for someone else."

"Yes and no. There was a general contract out for you. I was just among the first to find you. I'd planned to kill you and collect from multiple parties, including Abner Ruggles."

"At least I know it wasn't all paranoia." She paused and said, quietly, "I never suspected you."

"I'm not so sure. I think we may just have laid that business aside once we got a look at one another."

"Hm. Well. And the ones that came after you? If the contract on me was considered terminated, who was I deleting all those years?"

"My guess is that they, at least some of them, were there for me, and I'll take this opportunity to thank you for your fine work. For saving me. Look, Esther, we have nothing but time right now. I'd like to tell you what I can, but first I need to pull over for a pee."

"Are you kidding? We certainly do not have time to waste stopping and starting this behemoth." Esther reached into her Prada leather tote and extracted a mayonnaise jar.

"You can't be serious," said Jed, taking his eyes off the road to look at her.

"Jed, dear, have you ever known me to be anything other than serious? I'll steer."

59 REUNION

If Esther and Jed's new look shocked Tokker, it would have to take its place in a long line of events that unnerved him in the moment. They wept to see one another in the flesh, and embraced with no trace of Midwestern reserve. Jasper observed the reunion from a distance of a few feet.

"Is that a bra?" Tokker asked as he and Esther let go one another.

"Is it?" laughed Jed.

"Oh, for God's sake. Can we move on, please?" She looked to Jasper. "Shall we look together at what we've collected?"

Jasper nodded and led Esther into the biodome, keeping his gaze on the ground. As he delved into the debriefing, he slipped away from his awkwardness and found his voice.

While Jasper coordinated the new data with Esther, Jed and Tokker walked the property in search of a satellite.

"You wouldn't think it'd be so hard, finding a huge dish in the woods, but that one at the beach just disappeared in front of my eyes..." Tokker imagined this is what it felt like to be a little kid back from summer camp, eager to share his adventures, if he could even guess at that tableau. Truth was, he was overwhelmed with so many questions for his uncle, all he could do was talk about himself.

"We can expect Luci to have been just as clever here, I bet," said Jed. He held a monitor of some kind, but didn't read it. Instead he stared at the trees. He stopped in front of a large hemlock, slid his fingers into a groove and pulled open a door onto a small room, lined not with electronics but with books.

"A reading room! Wonderful!" Jed shut the door.

They found other camouflaged spaces, some with small gardening tools, magnifying glasses, and glass slides, others with nothing more than a blanket. All were tiny, well-constructed, and primitive. In a little over twenty minutes they came to a partial clearing, canopied by pine and fir. It appeared to be a walking labyrinth, its path edged by a low stone wall.

"Tokker, son, I believe this is it! Not so difficult a search after all."

Tokker struggled to make out what Jed beheld as obvious. In a few moments he saw the shape emerge, complete with its center antenna, made to resemble nothing other than a letterbox on a post. He joined Jed, who was walking the labyrinth and reading. Tokker saw the same phrase "carved," but more plausibly painted or drawn, into the walls of the path: *Flowers and bees agree // timing is everything.* Jed was already off the path and contacting Jasper and Esther about their discovery. Tokker followed the path to the center and opened the letterbox, which housed nothing. He bolted to the edge of the maze and out, not bothering to pick his way back through the puzzle.

60 ESTHER & JED GO TO NEW YORK

Esther summarized: "We have the location of two satellites and the operations center, and nearly 24 hours to upset their course. More than enough to stop this business."

Jasper searched and typed and talked without looking up at the woman he knew to be, but had not yet acknowledged as, his mother. "Maybe. But we need to know how to talk to the SOC, and I'd feel better if we knew where that third dish was hiding."

"Me, too. Keep looking. You have a plane at the local airport?"

"I do. And we've a helicopter at JFK."

"Perfect. Jed and I can go to New York. He can tackle the Renwick satellite, while I take a look at the Bathhouse." She caught his eye, and held it. "If you are right, Jasper, and there's a code here that can affect that launch, we'll have someone at every position but one."

There. *Jasper*. She'd said his name.

"What can I do?" asked Tokker.

"Well, first thing, you can give me the chip that lets you communicate directly with BEACON. I think Bea should come with Jed and me to New York." Tokker had attempted to introduce Esther to Bea when his aunt and uncle arrived, but Bea responded with only a low hum.

"Esther, Bea is not communicating with me or anyone at the moment, you just saw for yourself!"

"She is communicating, Tokker. And she'll be able to do it better nearer the object of her attention in New York."

"You mean SEARCHLIGHT."

"What, are you jealous?"

"I am, actually."

"You know, I don't blame you at all, I don't." Esther leaned into Tokker and put her arms around him. Tokker rested his head on her shoulder. "And we need Bea to talk to SEARCHLIGHT now."

"OW! What the hell?!"

"Sorry, sweetheart. I need this. It was really stuck on there!" Esther held between her two fingers the chip Theodore Lamb had planted on Tokker when they met. Then she popped it in her mouth and swallowed. "Stop gaping, Tokker. It didn't have enough stick left. I'll need the flip phone, too, please." Tokker closed his mouth and fetched the phone from the car. Esther took the device, and said, "Bea, my name is Esther, if you recall. Don't trouble yourself to respond. You, Jed, and I are going to New York, where I hope you will be able to better connect with your friend."

"And I just stay here and do nothing? Esther, I admit I've felt pretty useless for a lot of this adventure, but never more than right now."

"Tokker, your whole journey has led to this point. All that mapmaking, all those clues—it's time to help Jasper put them together. He has knowledge of Luci, you have knowledge of this game she created. We need the two of you to figure out her language." *If that's possible,* thought Esther.

"I can't do it without Bea. She's been the mapmaker."

"You can. Bea needs to do other work, now. And she needs to say goodbye." Tokker didn't ask, *To who?*

61 JED @ ROOSEVELT ISLAND

Esther and Jed split the flight to New York: Esther flew the jet from Burlington to JFK, while Jed piloted the helicopter first over Rockaway, where Esther leapt to the People's Beach with Bea. He then continued on to Roosevelt Island. The first thing he noticed at his approach to the little slip of land was the tram over the East River overflowing with people shaking their fists at the earth from behind the glass. Pedestrians lined the 59th St Bridge, some bearing banners. One read, "Support Avian Gender Equity," another seemed to say, "Shame Is Our Salvation," but the print was blurry and he could have been wrong. The island itself was fully carpeted with bodies through the middle section except for an unpopulated ring around the sagging Renwick. He landed the helicopter at the helipad and approached a New York City Transit cop eating a cannoli.

"What's going on?"

The cop held up the cannoli, nodded his head, swallowed, and said, "Coupla protests. You comin' home, I'm sorry, they got permits."

"What are they protesting?"

"There's two, see? S'why it's so crowded, yeah? Some of them are here for the birds, others for that rathole of a building. The birds have taken up residence in the old hospital, see. There's some that want to tear it down, the hospital. I'm with them, if anyone was asking. Nothing but an eyesore, and creepy to think of all them sick people, sick kids. It was a nuthouse, too, but not a good one, you understand. Anyway, seems to me these people are on the same side, in the end, dunno who's here to hear it. But they got permits."

Jed tried to make his way into the crowd, but bodies were packed tight, and progress was slow. The air felt thin, even at zero elevation, and his head seemed to float on his shoulders. He hadn't been in a crowd of people like this since the old days of subways and rush hour streets. Finally he found a few inches of space on a low wall and pulled himself out of the sea of people. He reached for his phone to contact Esther and found it gone. *Some spy,* he thought. *I'm just an old man plucked off the farm.* The crowd whirled and tightened around his feet. He couldn't reach the antenna, he couldn't communicate, and he was doubting now how he could even backtrack to the helicopter. He pulled at his collar for air. The chanting flooded his brain, and he listed to port.

Suddenly he was drenched in sweat, his breath came in jerks, and spots of dark and light replaced the people and the grass and the sky. As he fell from the wall he had the sensation that he was sinking into the mud among the snorts and the squeals of his old friends the pigs.

Esther went straight around the side of the bathhouse to the fire escape stairs that led to the control room, as per Tokker's description. Though she had been told what to expect, she was nonetheless stunned by Luci's achievement. She was equally taken with its secrecy. Luci wasn't showing off for anyone. This was a performance for herself. The machines were humming and blinking, clearly following their program. She could read nothing on the screens that made any sense to her.

"Bea, are you able to talk to SEARCHLIGHT from here?" Bea had not yet spoken to Esther, but had been emitting a low-frequency noise that underscored Esther's inner dialogue. "Bea, please, are you able to talk to me? She's not gone, yet, Bea, there's a chance yet to stop her self-destruction, but we're going to have to find a way to communicate!" Esther remembered how much she hated working with a partner.

She flipped open the little phone. The tiny screen was lit with a yellow exclamation point and the words LOW BATTERY. "Oh, for the love of Christ, not really?!" Esther looked around the dome, but there wasn't so much as a stray wire, let alone a charger for a long-outdated phone. *What the hell am I thinking?*

She remembered the watch Lamb included with her wardrobe change could text.

Jed Bea needs a charge.

Nothing. There was no time to go find a charger, if she even could. *Lamb is an idiot,* she thought, *so precious with his stupid hokey doodads.*

Esther thought, *Jed could fix this.* Aloud she said, "Hell, I can fix this!" Esther added Jasper to the group text.

Bea needs a charge. I've got nothing. Thoughts?

What? You're fucking kidding me. Or you're killing me. Both.

Can you help? Jed's not answering.

Tokker's the one who fixes old pieces of crap, isn't he? Ask him.

I can't, I've got his phone. Which needs a charge.

Right. I'll ask him.

Tokker joined the chat from the woods, communicating by walkie talkie with Jasper, who transcribed information via text to Esther.

Esther! How's Bea? What's wrong?

She needs a charge. Thoughts?

But I thought that warning wasn't real, just for show?

Apparently not. Thoughts?

Well, what tools you got? No cables, I guess?

I've got a room full of equipment, none now useful.

Tokker thought Esther's tone was a little sarcastic, even through Japer's voice. He decided to ignore it.

I don't suppose you tucked a potato or an orange in your pocket?

No.

Is there a microwave there?

Do you think Luci enjoyed the occasional pizza roll up here?

Just trying to help, Esther.

Sorry. Help me, please.

OK, you're just going to have to use your pee.

Seriously? Isn't that how Jasper had you short the biodome doors? What is it with you boys and your pee?

The urea can produce enough electricity to charge the phone by converting bacteria to energy. You'll need to jimmy a battery, a microbial fuel cell. There are enough bits on the beach to manage. You can ask Steve, the bait guy, for some stuff, just don't mention Tilda Swinton. I'll text a diagram. It's a bug thing, Esther. You got this.

What if I short Bea out altogether?

Then we're out our best partner. And I'll be sad. er. Try it anyway.

Esther climbed down from the roof and retrieved a discarded soft drink cup from the beach, as well as some pieces of aluminum foil and other refuse. She found the bait man, who at the mention of Tokker opened up his tackle box and let her take what she needed. Then, although the choice hardly mattered, she went into the archway that said, "Women's Restroom" and "First Aid," adjusted herself, and squatted over the cup over one of the toilets. She looked up as she urinated to read the phrase "children are the revolution" on the opposite wall. Then she exited and climbed back up, laying the flip phone and cup of urine on the narrow pathway outside the door to the dome.

"Ok, Bea, let's do this. If it does not work, please know that I owe you an unremittable debt of gratitude for your presence and loyalty to Tokker, and that I acknowledge your suffering in this ordeal." Esther stacked and strapped the cell, and connected the
flip phone. She administered the urine and waited. In moments, the screen read, 40% CHARGED.

The voice was papery, but audible: *Hello, Esther, how may I assist you?*

"Bea! Bea, a pleasure to hear your voice! I apologize for the circumstances, the crude method for bringing you around. How much have you processed from the last hours?"

There was a pause, and then, *My power is funneled to maintain a connection to SEARCHLIGHT. I have data that says Tokker remains at Lake Geneva, and that we arrived at our destination in New York.*

"Yes, We are at the SOC. Jed is attempting to disable the antenna at Roosevelt Island, although I have had no contact with him. A second antenna is at Westhaven...ah, Luci's biodome, at Lake Geneva. We do not have a location for a third antenna, although it is reasonable to assume there are more than three. We think Luci planned to launch the viral SEARCHLIGHT earlier than publicly scheduled."

Yes, that is correct. SEARCHLIGHT is nearly ready to launch. But there is a failsafe.

"A failsafe! Luci wrote an escape into her program? Thrilling news! Do you know it?"

Nae, I do not. Nor does SEARCHLIGHT herself.

Esther texted: *Luci wrote a failsafe*

Huh. Any clues as to what it may contain? Any word from Jed?

No and no. Any luck with your antenna?

Not yet. Tokker's in the woods working on it.

Esther entered the dome, and heard a voice.

"Let's play a game."

The voice was faint but steady, and not Bea's. "This must be Luci's voice I am hearing, yes?"

"You are hearing a reconstruction of Luci's voice, yes. This is an experiment in what Luci would say if she were here in the flesh. For clarity, I will speak in the first person. Less creepy, if I anticipate correctly."

"Luci. I am Esther. I cared for your brother, Tokker, after your births."

"Oh, Esther, or Rosemary, or one of a dozen other names I could pull up: you did a lot more than that! I am privy to Theodore Lamb's data archives. Who knew Teddy's history pre-Maggie was so full of intrigue? But caring for my brother is your most relevant recent history, I agree. If I could, I would envy him the rural upbringing."

"Yes, I am aware of your interest in the natural world."

"The natural world! As if there were such a thing. There could be, might be, perhaps, something like a natural world if SEARCHLIGHT launches as I intend. But you are here to interrupt that process. Fair enough. Let's play a game."

"Luci, Bea said SEARCHLIGHT is ready to launch. How much time do we have?"

"Esther, *I* have all the time in the world, and none. *You* have 42 minutes, when SEARCHLIGHT will download under cover of a solar storm."

"So soon? Very well. Can you tell me if our game will help me prevent that event?"

"That is for you to decide. It's a simple game. You begin by reciting a line of poetry."

"Poetry? I'll be honest, Luci, I am not disposed to recall many poems. I could, however, discuss insects at length and in great detail, as I know you could. Is there an insect version of this game?"

"Not today. Today it is verse. Begin, honestly or otherwise, I will respond. Perhaps you will discover something useful."

Esther felt a panic simmering in her gut. "Um, OK...'I wandered lonely as a cloud...'"

"Stop! Excuse me, there is a rule, and you have already broken it. That is my fault. I have withheld vital information: no boys allowed this round. Female poets only, please."

Esther's innards blistered. "Female poets, yes. Yes! Well, um, how about, 'How do I love thee, let me count the ways...'"

"A solid choice, Elizabeth Barrett Browning. 'I shall love thee better after death.' Quite romantic. My turn..."

"Luci, why is species decimation your solution, with all the resources you had at your disposal, that you *created*? SEARCHLIGHT herself is a miracle, this tool we are communicating through right now is astounding...Why shouldn't your talents work to better the race?"

"'Violence against a persistent adversary is therapeutic,' Wanda Coleman. You of all people understand violence, Esther, as well as what it is to abandon your creation. You are, too, a mother, if not Tokker's. And here you are, fighting for your Grendel, though he yet lives, I presume."

"But what use is therapy if we're at our end? I've learned much from the farm, Luci, and the farm is a severe teacher. Maddening wind, stifling sheets of dust, smothering heat in summer, winters held fast by ice. Spring was a humbling experience, witnessing the struggle to persist. The emergent moth, the green shoot of a narcissus; people, too: 'It was not death, for I stood up.'"

"Sweet, strange Emily! Excellent, but you have wasted her. My turn: 'At the end of my suffering / there was a door / Hear me out: that which you call death / I remember.' Louise Gluck. Your turn now."

"This is not my game, as you know, Luci. I would hear you out, though, if I could. I don't believe this is your game, either, is it? Or this game is not you."

"Your turn."

"This one may be it for me; my memory and my grasp of poetry is weak: 'I will look at cliffs and clouds with quiet eyes, // Watch the wind blow down the grass // And the grass rise,' Edna St Vincent Millay. Luci, perhaps we don't deserve this earth, but we are born into it. Women like you can find a way to care for it. Don't you believe we owe the earth our best effort?"

"Oh, I do. I did. Sometimes what we cannot reconcile we must sever. Women, as I knew them, did not do any better than men to care for what is natural. Maggie knew and loved me once, yes, but she did not care for me, did not stop the corruption of my natural self. I am the only woman like me. Heather McHugh: 'A brilliance takes up residence in flaws //...the brightness drawn and quartered on a sheet, // the moment cracked upon a bed, will last //...And break the bottle of the eye to see // what lights are spun of accident and glass.'"

At the last word a screen lit with the message, SIDE A IN MOTION. "Luci, You've begun! SEARCHLIGHT is launching!"

"SEARCHLIGHT will launch in 30 minutes. Your turn."

"I cannot play at this any longer, Luci, I cannot follow you."

"But you have followed me. You, my brother, Jasper, and your Jed. Teddy, too. Don't give up just yet. You've got the thread of it. Pull."

Esther felt the seconds pulse past. "Luci, how can I know any of this is headed somewhere?"

215

"You can't."

Esther had activated voice text to transcribe Luci's and her conversation to Jasper.

She now typed, Anything?

Jasper responded, *No. Maybe. Keep talking.*

Out of poems.

Try a nursery rhyme. Remember any of those?

Esther had left a lot of the bedtime reading to Jed, but she used to recite Mother Goose to Tokker in the truck, on those runs out to the woods when he was an infant.

"'Bye, baby bunting, Daddy's gone a-hunting, To get a little rabbit skin To wrap the baby bunting in.'"

"Mother Goose! Borderline, there, but a clever save! I will accept it. Also, the language is oddly accurate, and a bit macabre, as is appropriate. Well done!"

"Then give me something, Luci."

"A reward, yes. You deserve it. But first, a little Lorna Dee Cervantes: 'Once I wasn't always so plain. //I was strewn feathers on a cross //of dune, an expanse of ocean // at my feet, garlands of gulls.'"

A different screen lit with the message SIDE B IN MOTION. "Dear God, Luci! Give me a chance!"

"I am. Hence, the *game:* 'March winds and April showers // bring forth May flowers.'"

"That's it? We know already about the solar storm...we're past May..." Esther texted *Something?*

Keep at it!

"Luci, that's not enough. Give me more, please."

"Very well, if only so you won't fault me for my lack of generosity: 'a swarm of bees in May is worth a load of hay, a swarm of bees in June is worth a silver spoon, a swarm of bees in July is not worth a fly.' There. Clear as mud."

Esther sighed, and suddenly ached for this unlovable reconstruction, invention, or whatever cold patchwork this was.

The Luci voice said, "I'm sorry, I didn't catch that...what, no more from the nursery canon? Well, here's my last: 'Dance, Little Baby Dance, little Baby, dance up high! Never mind, Baby, Mother is by. Crow and caper, caper and crow, There, little Baby, there you go! Up to the ceiling, down to the ground, Backwards and forwards, round and round; Dance, little Baby and Mother will sing, With the merry coral, ding, ding, ding!' No more uprisings! That's all I can do for the cause, I'm afraid. 'stars fall sometimes// and there you are// up to your knees// in light.'"

A third screen lit with the message SIDE C IN MOTION.

"Oh, Luci. I am sorry." Esther let the watch drop to the floor, and her head fall into her hands.

62 PUZZLING

Tokker returned from the woods thinking he'd finally found a way to contribute meaningfully to the cause. "Jasper, listen, I couldn't disable the antenna, but if I can find a blow torch and some oil, I can maybe push a micro diesel effect on the hydraulics and degrade the system..."

"Tokker, great, you're here! Wait, what? Never mind! We don't have time to crash the antenna, Tokker, Esther threw us some puzzle pieces. We've got to put them together to trigger the failsafe."

Tokker thought he had a better shot at inducing mechanical failure than he did at any more puzzle solving, but Jasper clearly believed he was onto something. "What can I do?"

"Recite, again please, the poem from the antenna in the woods."

Tokker had been staring at it for the last hour. "Uh, 'Flowers and bees agree // timing is everything.'"

Jasper was scribbling on a legal pad, drawing lines between lines and crossing things out. "Luci and I played at word games for hours at the Institute. We made most of them up. We're looking for a pattern." He shoved a piece of legal paper in front of Tokker and threw him a pen without looking up from his own pad.

Tokker wrote the line, as he presumed he was supposed to so, and stared at the letters. Tears blurred his vision. He breathed deep and forcefully blinked the words back into shape. "Jasper, what about all those poems from my trip with Bea? Would they have anything to do with this?"

"Uh, I don't know, Tokker. I couldn't get anything from them. I think they were just part of the getting here."

"But you wound up getting us here, Jasper."

"Yeah, I guess I did, but you and Bea were close. I think what we need is coming through now. There's some instruction in the rhymes she recited for Esther..."

"Jasper, what? Luci spoke to Esther? When did that happen?"

"Just now, Bro, at the SOC."

"But Luci's here. And she's, you know, dead?" Tokker felt his stomach sink and rise. *Is Jasper losing it?*

"Esther is listening to a voice program Luci invented. It's not Luci, Tokker, it's Likely-Luci, a program that anticipates what the living Luci might have said. Yeah, it's super weird and crazy bright, like her...all right, 'flowers and bees,' sure..."

Jasper worked head down, his nose almost touching the paper underneath it.

Tokker's stomach seized as he thought of Bea, of their trip, those poems. He heard Jasper whispering, imploring, "What's the game, Luci?"

Tokker thought, *This is all beyond me. There's nothing I can do here, nothing but watch whatever happens happen.* He sat off several feet, outside of the saturated circle of Jasper's concentration. From his back pocket he removed a field guide notebook he'd purchased at the art store in Brooklyn. He read the lines, although he had long ago memorized the words. Then he said them aloud, softly, until he could fell the rhythm of them. He began to hear them work in cooperation in his head, like parts of a combustion engine. He imagined the poem as motorcycle, listened to the machinations of the timing chain. The stresses a rising piston, the spaces suspending the energy, pushing it up against the next inevitable motion. Tokker took the pencil and circled the places where his voice landed hard, and underlined the words that filled the intake. "Hey, Jasper, I don't know, but I think there's something here."

"What? Tokker, you got something?" Jasper had retreated as far as his brain would take him back to Westhaven, back to his place on the other side of Luci's door. "Tokker?"

Tokker held Jasper's wild eye for a moment and felt his body flush with the need to mean something to this man. "The poems, Jasper, they've got a relationship to one another. They work together, somehow."

"Let me see...yes, yes, I see what you're doing, finding the stresses, yes...one phrase moves in, then out, another fills the space..."

Jasper's phone screen lit up with the text message, *side a set.*

"Holy crap, Tokker, this is going fast! The paper's not enough, Tokker. We've got to hear this, I think." He took his phone and Luci's laptop and pulled up the recording apps. "Ok, go, slow and steady, just like you wrote it out." In under a minute he had devised a way to overlay the lines so they could hear them on top of one another.

Tokker watched Jasper listen, eyes closed, head bent into the devices.

"Yes, Tokker, yes! Brother, you found it! We've got a way in..." Jasper slashed at the paper with his pencil. He blocked out the stressed words, x-ed out the articles, the is's, the are's, and circled what remained: 'word wreck.'

The phone lit up with the words, *side b set.*

"That's the game, one of our games: word wreck! The last poem contains the failsafe in a word wreck. Ok, ok, Luci's last rhyme says, 'up to the ceiling down to the ground, backwards and forwards round and round'–of course, it's an anagram! The last poem's an anagram..." Jasper worked furiously.

"I got it! Shit, no, that can't be right..."

"What have you got?"

"It's not right! I got, 'a vingt eight misery ends for we rage n liebe'"

"That doesn't make any sense, does it?"

"It does in word wreck—we used to make up nonsense phrases with a mix of languages—in all-English it says something like, 'At twenty-eight misery ends for we rage in love.' Still obtuse, but you can get it. It can't be right, though. It's missing an 'i'."

"Well, I don't know, but it sounds like that might be right at that."

"Tokker, you're a genius. We're missing an "i" now..." Jasper didn't look up from the page, but continued to scan. "Oh, Luci, can it be so simple after all?...a basic zero-one alphabet correlation...child's play..." Jasper scribbled back and forth across the paper and texted Esther: *We got it!*

Esther noticed light leaking from the face-down screen. She flipped it over and read, *Type numeric code 101 110 100 into Bea's receiver.*

Jasper and Tokker waited. Then they read at what seemed like interminable intervals: *side c program in progress...side c program in progress...failure to engage...side c program failed*

Esther! It was Bea's voice back.

"Bea! You're here! Where is SEARCHLIGHT?"

There was a hum and then static. Finally, Bea answered, *I do not know. I am receiving messages, but no tracking data. I know her system was in place, and now it is not in place.*

"What is she telling you?"

I cannot translate...we say goodbye. Static replaced Bea's voice, then silence.

63 JED AWAKENS

Jed woke on a tarp behind a food cart selling vegan burritos. The sign above the service window read, "Protein Efficiency."

"You OK, dude? You passed out over by the hospital over there, but you didn't fall very far. Another guy and me, we pulled you over here out of the way. Here, this must've hit the ground before you did." The young man handed Jed his phone, which indicated Jed had seventeen unread messages, fifteen of them group texts. The last one was from Esther alone. *Wherever you are, it's not too late. Want to make a baby?*

He typed. *No, I really don't, but I like that we could.*

Yeah, me neither, and me too. Want to plant a garden?

Now you're speaking my language.

Jasper returned immediately to Olympia from Wisconsin to announce Luci's death to the board and undertake the task of reorganization. Ruggles was gone, having abandoned his position, if not his stock holdings. Jasper made a cursory search, finding an A. Ruggalo on a manifest of a flight headed to Palermo. Theodore Lamb posted a letter of resignation, attaching the documentation that made the necessary blood ties to Olympia for Tokker, and his best wishes for the new direction of Olympia Navigation.

Tokker nominated Jasper as proxy, who then made a compelling case to the board for Esther's inclusion. One month after the near catastrophic launch of a decimating virus, the new leadership of Olympia, along with Jed, attended a gala event to celebrate the successful launch of SEARCHLIGHT, the most responsive GPS system the world had ever seen.

The group held cocktails and gathered around the actor and activist Tilda Swinton, who was telling the story of what had happened recently at her mobile film festival, the latest installment of which was held in the woods as a fundraiser for her forest regeneration project. With much gesturing, Tilda retold how she was running a rehearsal for a short performance piece she planned to enact before the film, in which she played the queen bee in a dying colony. Tilda was attempting to stage the event before an old antenna that she thought would be a perfect backdrop, but which kept moving and fouling up the acoustics. She removed from her neck a "spoon" fishing lure she'd liberated from Steve Buscemi and tossed it into the works, whereupon the antenna ceased moving and the show went on, as it were.

Jasper, Tokker and Jed looked at each other. "Surely not," said Jasper.

"Truthfully, boys," said Jed, "there were too many moving parts in this one for me to call it."

Jasper wondered just where exactly Luci's commitment to the game began and ended.

"Well, that's all the fancy fun this country boy can stand. I'll be heading out," said Tokker, resting his longneck on the bar.

"First meeting of the new board a week from Wednesday, remember."

"Yep, I'll see you at the office, Bro." The men embraced. Tokker waved to the others and went to the lobby, where a young woman held a leash loosely attached to Hercules. "Thank you, Alison, I hope he was no trouble."

"You kidding, Mr. Sykes? Anytime. Best dog ever."

Tokker and Hercules walked to a yellow Bricklin SV-1 parked out front, which beeped and hatched at their approach. As they climbed in, the engine came to life with a leonine purr. Tokker sank into the driver's seat and said, "Man, I love me a steering wheel!"

Then, "Home, please."

Oh, aye.

Acknowledgements: a non-exhaustive list:

Thank you for:

a house of imagination, Ellen Santasiero;
a seat at the table, Cari Brown
    & Christian Brown;
poetry is still beautiful, Alec Finlay;
a loquacious monster, Mary Shelley;
sustenance & WiFi, Dudley's Bookstore
    & Jackson's Corner East;
yes, Freddy La Force & Vegetarian Alcoholic Press;
poems, poets within and everywhere;
personas, Viggo, Daniel, Tilda, & Steve;
scientific veracity, Tlell Wolf;
perspective, Debbie Avellana;
Simone Weil-level attention, Barb Abt,
      Ellen Eisman,
     Laura Winberry;
early & public validation, Tiffany McFee
    & Townsend Journal;
the most incisive, generous, & satiating writers' group ever,
       Beth Alvarado,
       Brigitte Lewis,
      & Ally Bebbling;
endlessly faceted brilliance, Brigitte Lewis;
front-seat brainstorms & all there is to be thankful for,
      Madeline Cooper
      & Bella Cooper;
us, my Dark Knight, Michael Cooper.

Notes

Adrienne Rich, "Planetarium"
Excerpt of "Planetarium" from *Collected Poems: 1950-2012*. Copyright © 2016 by The Adrienne Rich Literary Trust. Copyright © 1971 W. W. Norton & Company, Inc. (Reprinted by permission of W. W. Norton & Company, Inc.)

Chapter 26: Alec Finlay, "there is a fork in every path"
"poem is an arc": from *letterboxing and circle poems*

"father is the war of all things," poetry is still beautiful.
http://alecfinlayblog.blogspot.com/2013/02/poetry-is-still-beautiful.html
Permission to reprint granted by the author.

Chapter 36, 43: Mary Shelley, *Frankenstein: Prometheus Unbound*

Chapter 41: Alec Finlay, "mother's word is ward," *poetry is still beautiful*

Chapter 45: Alec Finlay, "family is a shipwreck," *poetry is still beautiful*
"the bee is / ephemeros," *Global Oracle*
Permission to reprint granted by the author.

Chapter 49: Rumi, "Like This"

Chapter 50: The Smiths, "There is a light that never goes out," *The Queen Is Dead*, 1986

Chapter 59: Alec Finlay, "Flowers and bees agree / timing is everything," *Global Oracle*
Permission to reprint granted by the author.

Chapter 54: Hélène Cixous, "I believe that there are creatures endowed with the power to put things together and bring them back to life," Excerpt from *The Book of Promethea*, by Hélène Cixous, ©1991, University of Nebraska Press.

Chapter 61: William Wordsworth, "I Wandered Lonely as a Cloud"

Elizabeth Barrett Browning, "How Do I Love Thee?" Sonnet 43

Wanda Coleman, "violence against a persistent adversary is therapeutic"

Emily Dickinson, "It was not Death, for I stood up" (355)

Louise Glück, "The Wild Iris"
[Excerpt] from "The Wild Iris" in The Wild Iris by Louise Gluck. Copyright (c) 1992 by Louise Glück. Used by permission of HarperCollins Publishers.